ADMINISTRATIVE ETHICS

PAPER-III - UNIT-III (PART-A)

For R.A.S. Mains Examination

R.K. Sirohi

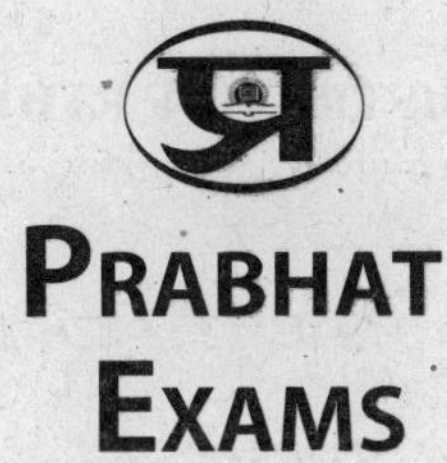

PRABHAT EXAMS

Publisher
PRABHAT EXAMS
Imprint of Prabhat Prakashan Pvt. Ltd.
4/19 Asaf Ali Road, New Delhi–110 002
Ph. 23289555 • 23289666 • 23289777 • Helpline/ 7827007777
e-mail: prabhatbooks@gmail.com • Website: www.prabhatbooks.com

Price
Two Hundred Ninety Five only

ISBN 978-93-5322-126-3

Printed at
Sita Fine Arts Pvt. Ltd., New Delhi

ADMINISTRATIVE ETHICS
by R.K. Sirohi

ISBN 978-93-5322-126-3

₹ 295.00

Contents

Ethics of Administration

1

CHAPTER

With the passage of time, the concept of civil service has been reformed as well as ideas of its role and responsibilities. The comprehensive civil service structure and established practices of Independent India came down from the administration system of the British India. Its usefulness for confirming national unity as well as better administration in the country was marked by Sardar Vallabhbhai Patel and granted by the Constituent Assembly and incorporated in the Constitution. ***It is appropriate currently to recollect the Sardar's insight and his vision:***

'I need hardly emphasize that an efficient, disciplined and contented service, assured of its prospects as a result of diligent and honest work, and is sine qua non of sound administration under a democratic regime even more than under an authoritarian rule. The service must be above party and we should ensure that political considerations either in its recruitment or in its discipline and control are reduced to the minimum, if not eliminated altogether'.

ADMINISTRATIVE ETHICS

A set of principles, norms and rules of behaviour, moral values and moral requirements are called administrative ethics. In the domain of public administration, these are applicable to persons who act as professional managers. Ethics is a branch of philosophy which seeks to address morality. In the public sector, ethics addresses the fundamental premise of a public administrator's duty as a "steward" to the public. Ethics is the moral consideration and justification for decisions made and actions taken in time for completion of daily responsibilities while working to provide the general services of government and non-profit organizations.

It is generally emphasized that the employees of the government establish ethical standards for managerial decisions, analyse these standards and bear personal and professional accountability for the decisions made. **"A set of moral norms and requirements for those in public administration targeting their professional activity at attainment of common wealth and effective use of moral values" is considered Civil service ethics.**

The objective of civil service ethics is keeping the essence and content of professional activities approved socially and to regulate employee relations by dint of norms, behaviour and actions, and to form an ethical ingredient element in the consciousness of public administration employees.

The moral norms are the basis of Civil service ethics. The Latin word 'norm' implies rule and pattern. This being one of the easiest types of ethical requirement and is utilized as an element of ethical relations and as a type of ethical consciousness.

THE ETHICS OF ADMINISTRATION CONSIST OF THREE BASIC COMPONENTS

1. ***Standards and norms:*** The actions of people and employees are guided by certain principles which help in leading and controlling their behaviour, fore example, formulation of laws, codes and rules.
2. ***Values:*** These are the individuals, group and social statements, opinions and attitudes towards concepts such as justice, freedom, responsibility, loyalty, neutrality, honesty, etc.
3. ***Behaviour:*** It depends on the different kinds of employee actions limited by particular standards and norms relating to social values.

SPECIFIC ETHICAL REQUIREMENTS FOR THE CIVIL SERVICE

Ethical requirements for civil servants are determined by various methods described as follows:

1. They reflect the ideas and objectives of the civil service and certain tasks of different governmental institutions.
2. The conception of an ideal or targeted public administration model adopted in society influence these principles. A civil society is the source of administrative ethics, as its requirements, concerns and expectations are highlighted in ethical norms and requirements.

Administrative ethics should perform the following fundamental tasks:

- Taking part in the regulation of the relationship between government and citizens
- Promoting public and state concerns in government activities in the maximum possible manner
- Providing public administration staff with certain behavioural standards on the basis of morality.

REQUIREMENT FOR ADMINISTRATIVE ETHICS

The civil service of the nation was regarded as the chief agent of socio-economic change. It has brought about a notable shift after independence in mid-sixties. The administrators were demonstrating disinterest and lack of promise to the socio-economic initiatives of the legislature. In this regard, the remark of the Prime Minister Rajiv Gandhi on the administrative culture are as follows:

"......and what of the iron frame of system, the administrative services.....and the myriad functionaries of the state...but as the proverb says there can be no protection if the fence starts eating the crop. This is what has happened. The fence has started eating grass... we have government servants who do not serve but oppress the poor and the helpless....who don't uphold the law...but connive with those who cheat the state....they have no work ethic, no feeling for the public cause, no involvement in the future of the nation. They have only a grasping mercenary outlook, devoid of competence, integrity and commitment..."

The Indian government held a conference of chief secretaries in 1996 with a view to developing an agenda for fruitful and responsive administration to ensure responsive, responsible, transparent, decentralized and public-friendly administration from top to bottom. An action plan of Effective and Accountable Administration was put before the Conference of Chief Ministers held in 1997. Three major areas of action plan discussed in the conference were as follows:

1. Making administration accountable and citizen friendly;
2. Confirming transparency and right to information and
3. Motivating civil services.

The Fourth Report of Second Administrative Reform Commission on Ethics in Governance emphasized on the need of developing special set of values for public service. The commission observed:

"Public Service Values' towards which all public servants should aspire, should be defined and made applicable to all tiers of Government and parastatal organizations. Any transgression of these values should be treated as misconduct, inviting punishment."

Ethics: The In-Depth Human Interface

2 CHAPTER

Ethics is that segment of philosophy, which includes standardizing, safeguarding and proposing concepts of right and wrong conduct. It is also known as moral philosophy. Derived from the Greek word ethos, the term ethics means "character". While it is a counterpart to Aesthetics in Axiology, in philosophy, ethics studies the moral behaviour in humans and the way they should act.

DOMAINS OF ETHICAL STUDY/BRANCHES OF ETHICS

There are Three Extensive Fields of Ethical Study

a. ***Meta-ethics***: The focus of this branch of ethics is on the meaning of ethical terms themselves (for instance, 'what is goodness?') and to get the answers to questions for attaining ethical knowledge, instead of focusing on the question of common usage. For example, it will focus on the nature of questions such as 'how can I distinguish what is good from what is bad?' instead of 'what should I do in a particular situation?' Thus, meta-ethics deals with the nature of ethical properties, attitudes, statements, and judgments. It studies such themes for exploring the meaning attached with moral questions and the basis for people to know what is 'true' or 'false'.

b. ***Normative ethics is*** that branch of ethics, which analyses the ethical acts. Thus, generally, it focuses absolutely on questions of 'what is the right thing to do?' It deals with questions of what people ought to do when faced in ambiguous situation, and on how to make decision on what 'correct' moral actions need to be taken.

c. ***Applied ethics*** deals with the way adopted by the people to achieve moral outcomes in specific situations. Hence, it takes into account the philosophical examination of peculiar and generally complex issues involving moral judgments. Applied ethics covers areas such as bioethics, business/corporate ethics, development ethics, and environmental ethics. However, discriminating between the normative and applied ethics is getting increasingly difficult.

META-ETHICS

Meta-ethics is that branch of ethics that deals with the nature of goodness and badness and what it is to be morally right or wrong instead of dealing with what acts or what kind of acts are good or bad, right or wrong, and thus it is regarded as the most abstract area of moral philosophy.

Meta-ethics is often associated with philosophical ethics, but in this specific sense, it became more noticeable with G.E. Moore's Principia Ethica from 1903. In Principia Ethica, he first describes about the naturalistic fallacy. In his open-question argument, Moore discarded naturalism in ethics. This caused the thinkers to reconsider the second order questions about ethics. The Scottish philosopher David Hume had expressed a similar opinion on the difference between facts and values, previously.

The biggest dispute in metaethics might be the difference of opinion that divides ***moral realists*** and ***antirealists.***

Moral realists are of the opinion that moral facts are objective facts that already exist in the world. Things termed as good or bad do not depend on our interpretation, and then we appear and discover morality.

Antirealists on the contrary are of the opinion that without our involvement in their interpretation, moral facts are non-existent in the world and that the facts about us determine the morality. Holding this viewpoint, morality is something, which is invented and not something that is discovered.

The disagreement between ***cognitivism and noncognitivism*** is quite close in relation to that of moral realists and antirealists..

Cognitivism holds the value that moral statements express the world. If a person considers lying as wrong, then in the cognitivist' viewpoint that person has said something about the world, and that person has assigned a property wrongness to an act of lying. It is an objective matter that whether lying has that property, and so the statement made by the person might objectively either true or false.

Non-cognitivists holds a contrary opinion and do not approve this analysis of moral statements. From the view point of noncognitivists, someone making moral statements are expressing their feelings or telling people what to do and are not describing the world. Non-cognitivism holds the opinion that moral statements are non-descriptive and are neither true nor false. It relates that for something to be true, it is described as being the way that it is, and to be false it is described as being other than the way that it is; statements that are not descriptive cannot be either.

NORMATIVE ETHICS

Normative ethics is that branch of philosophical ethics, which analyses the ethical acts. It enquires into the set of questions that emerge in view of how one ought to act. It is dissimilar to meta-ethics because it analyses the criteria for the rightness and wrongness of actions. Meta-ethics in comparison analyses the meaning of moral language and the metaphysics of moral facts. Normative ethics also differs from descriptive ethics, as the latter is an empirical study of people's moral beliefs. In other words, descriptive ethics would focus on determining the proportion of people who believe killing to be always wrong, whereas normative ethics focuses on whether holding such a belief is correct. Thus, normative ethics is sometimes referred to as prescriptive, rather than descriptive. However, the nature of moral facts could be both descriptive and prescriptive at the same time on certain versions of the meta-ethical view called moral realism.

APPLIED ETHICS

Applied ethics is that branch of philosophy that is concerned with application of ethical theory to real-life situations. The discipline is bifurcated into many specialized domains, such as engineering ethics, bioethics, geo ethics, public service ethics and business ethics.

Applied ethics finds usage in some facets of determining public policy, and is also used by individuals facing difficult decisions. It addresses questions such as: "What are human rights, and how do we determine them?" "Is affirmative action right or wrong?" "Is getting an abortion immoral?" "Is euthanasia immoral?" "Do animals also have rights?" and "Do individuals have the right to self-determine?" A more explicit question could be "If someone else can make better out of his/her life than I can, is it then morally justified to sacrifice myself for them if needed?" These questions are necessary to balance law, politics, and the practice of arbitration. In fact, no common assumptions could be made of all participants. Hence, it is a pre-requirement to formulate the questions prior to rights balancing. However, it is not necessary that all questions studied in applied ethics concern public policy only. For example, To make ethical judgments regarding questions such as, "Is lying always wrong?" and, "If not, in which situations is it permitted?" Generally, people feel more comfortable with dichotomies (two opposites). However, in ethics, there are multifaceted issue to look out for and the best-proposed actions should address many diverse areas at the same time. While making ethical decisions, answers are almost never a "yes or no", "right or wrong" statement. Many buttons are pushed to improve the overall condition so that it does not benefit any particular faction.

Contributions of Moral Thinkers and Philosophers From India and the World

3 CHAPTER

Much of the philosophy concerning Western World is grounded on the basis of thoughts and teachings of Socrates, Plato and Aristotle: the three renowned historic Greek philosophers.

The virtue ethics of Socrates, Plato, Aristotle, the Epicureans, and the Stoics were absolutely peculiar and in particular concerned with assisting an individual turn into a better character through self-improvement.

Virtue morality requires people to apprehend how to transform themselves into refined people. That implies people need to comprehend what is moral, how to stay inspired to be moral, and how to absolutely act ethically.

The values and moral style in cutting-edge Indian philosophy may be seen in philosophy of Gandhi, Vivekananda, Aurobindo, Rabindranath Tagore and Radhakrishnan. Most of the Indian brand of liberalistic values and ethics originate from the ancient Vedas, the Upanishads and the Bhagavad Gita.

MORAL THINKERS FROM THE WORLD

Socrates

Socrates was born in Athens around 469 BCE and lived during the period of the city's best cultural growth.

He did not maintain an official school and did not charge for his services. He was a famous visitor at neighbourly gatherings, and could frequently be viewed contending in opposition to illogical argument and bias anywhere humans assembled. Socrates had no sympathy with the hermit—he believed in rejoicing life. He observed fault with the Sophists, modern-day teachers who wereinclined on contending either side of any dispute and with whom he was normally wrongly correlated. Socrates considered truth, beauty, and justice to be having objective content, and that we are born with an innate knowledge of their presence. He educated his disciples to use their reasonable interpretation to rediscover skills they by this time had. He additionally assumed that an ethical existence brought happiness to men, and that this morality was something that could be transmitted via education. He himself liked to claim that he knew nothing, which was his way of declaring that he had no constant doctrine. Socrates asserted ignorance was referred to by the Greeks eironeia, Socratic sarcasm.

In the opinion of Socrates, the perfect lifestyles focuses on self-development, in particular, the quest of goodness, morality, legitimacy, uprightness and friendship.

His doctrine of the soul made him believe that all virtues converge into one, which is the good, or knowledge of one's authentic self and objectives through the direction of a lifetime. Knowledge successively rely on the nature or essence of things as they definitely are, because the fundamental types of things are more factual than their experienced exemplifications. This conception leads to a teleological view of the world that every variety partakes and leads to the highest form, the form concerning the good. Plato afterwards expanded this philosophy as primary according to his own philosophy. Socrates's opinion is frequently described as holding virtue and know-how to be identical, so that no person intentionally does wrong. Since virtue is identical with knowledge, it can be inculcated, however, not as a professional domain as the Sophists had professed to teach it. However, Socrates himself gave no conclusive answer to the way virtue can be absorbed.

Plato

Plato's beliefs and writings contributed a great deal to the organized discipline concerning ethics. Plato believed so much every human beings in some way favoured happiness. A person's moves do not continually create enjoyment; however, it is due to the fact people do not comprehend what their actions will yield. Happiness is an end result of a wholesome soul, however, ethical virtue makes up the wellbeing of the soul.

People operate not constantly petition after stand virtuous however that is because that function not understand so much moral continence produces happiness. However, Plato states that if a person is aware that ethical virtue results in happiness, he or she should behave in accordance to this knowledge. Being ethical ormoral, then, has its basis in know-how or reason. If a character is aware that virtue results in contentment but acts opposite to the idea, he or she is morally wrong, and evil conduct is the sign of a contaminated soul.

Plato said that nice men had to be those having the qualities of being just, temperate, courageous and wise. He was talking of ethical excellence in a reasonably comparable manner than that of Socrates. In his work, The Republic, he demonstrates all these characteristics. The rapport he gives between State, citizens and moral excellence; he states that for a State to be good, it has to permit, assist and also motivate people to be as upright as individuals; that upright residents have been those who were good as individuals and accordingly useful to the country; and that moral excellence, or Virtue, is the groundwork of each and every good society and the sole method to have great men direct other great men appropriately.

Platonic Idealism

In *The Republic*, his primary thesis concerning the ideal state, Plato considered that the physical world around a person is not real; it is continually altering and for this reason you can never express what it indeed is. There is a world of ideas which is a world of static and complete truth. This is actuality for Plato. Does such a world exist impartial of individual minds? Plato believed it did, and whenever we hold an idea, or view something with our mind's eye, we are using our mind to visualize of something in the ideal world.

- In the fable regarding the cave, originated by Plato, the world was like a cave, and an individual would solely observe shadows cast from the outside light, consequently the only actuality would be thoughts.

Aristotle

Aristotle was Plato's excellent student. Plato had a great influence on Aristotle, just as Socrates had on Plato. One of his best-known ideas was his conception of "The Golden Mean" — "avoid extremes," the consultation of temperance in entire things.

Aristotle concludes that (a) the appropriate object regarding virtue is complacency and (b) we can turn out to be smart through habit.

Aristotle labelled the virtues as ethical and intellectual. He recognized a few intellectual virtues, the most important of which were wisdom; sophia (theoretical wisdom) and phronesis (practical wisdom). The foremost ethical virtues recognized include:

- Prudence
- Justice
- Fortitude (Courage)
- Temperance

Aristotle contended that every ethical virtue was a mean (called golden mean) between two corresponding vices, one of excess and one of deficiency. For instance, courage is a virtue determined between the vices of cowardliness and imprudence.

Aristotle spoke of the noble citizen as being any individual who does what he is supposed to do as per the norms set by the regime and accomplish his social role. He noted that there could be noble men whichever were now not good citizen. He afterwards believed that being a noble citizen does not accomplish one a proper person.

DIFFERENCE BETWEEN PLATO AND ARISTOTLE

In Philosophy

Plato trusted that ideas had a widespread form, a perfect shape, which prompts his optimistic philosophy. Aristotle trusted that universal structures were not essentially ascribed to each object or idea, and that each occurrence of an object or an idea had to be investigated on its own. This perspective results in Aristotelian Empiricism. For Plato, thought experiments and reasoning would be sufficient to "demonstrate" an idea or set up the characteristics of an object, but Aristotle rejected this in favour of directobservation and experience.

- In rationale, Plato was more disposed to utilize inductive reasoning, while Aristotle utilized deductive reasoning. The syllogism, an essential unit of rationale (if A = B, and

B = C, at that point A = C), was produced by Aristotle. (Deductive rationale utilizes given data, premises or acknowledged general standards to achieve a demonstrated conclusion. Then again, inductive logic includes making speculations in light of conduct saw in particular cases.)

- Both Aristotle and Plato trusted considerations were better than the senses. Nonetheless, while Plato trusted the senses could trick a man, Aristotle expressed that the senses were required with a specific end goal to perfectly decide reality.
- A case of this distinction is the fable of the cave, produced by Plato. To him, the world resembled a cave, and a man would just observe shadows cast from the outside light, so the main reality would be musings. To the Aristotelian technique, the conspicuous arrangement is to leave the cave and encounter what is throwing light and shadows straightforwardly, instead of relying entirely on out-of-the-way or inner experiences.

In Ethics

- Plato was Socratic in his conviction that information is righteousness, all by itself. This implies to know the great is to do the great, i.e., that knowing the proper activity will prompt one naturally making the best decision; this suggested virtue could be educated by showing somebody appropriate from wrong, great from immoral. Aristotle expressed that comprehending what was correct was insufficient, that one needed to act in the best possible way—fundamentally, to make the propensity for doing great. This definition set Aristotelian morals on a practical plane, as opposed to the hypothetical one upheld by Socrates and Plato.
- For Socrates and Plato, astuteness is the fundamental virtue and with it, one can bind together all views into an entirety. Aristotle trusted that astuteness was righteous, however that accomplishing prudence was neither programmed nor did it give any unification (obtaining) of different virtues. To Aristotle, shrewdness was an objective accomplished simply after exertion, and unless a man thought and act admirably, different ideals would remain inapplicable.
- Socrates trusted that joy could be accomplished without morality, yet that this joy was base and carnal. Plato expressed that virtue was adequate for satisfaction, and there was no such thing as "moral luck" to distribute rewards. Aristotle trusted that virtue was essential for joy, however inadequate by itself, requiring sufficient social constructs to enable an upright individual to feel happy and satisfied.

In Political Hypothesis

- Plato felt that a person ought to incorporate his or her interests to that of society keeping in mind the end goal to accomplish an ideal type of government. His Republic expressed an idealistic culture where each of the three classes (philosophers, warriors and labourers) had its part, and administration was kept in the hands of those regarded best qualified for that duty, those of the "Philosopher Rulers."
- Aristotle viewed the fundamental political unit as the city (polis), which took preference over the family, which consecutively took preference over the person. Aristotle said that man was a political creature by nature and hence could not maintain a strategic

distance from the difficulties of governmental issues. In his view, politics works more as a life form than as a machine, and the part of the polis was not righteousness or monetary strength, but to make a space where its kin could live a decent life and execute delightful acts. Aristotle moved past political hypothesis to end up becoming the foremost political researcher, watching political practices with a specific end goal to devise amendments.

Immanuel Kant

Immanuel Kant (1724–1804) is a standout amongst the most prestigious philosophers ever. His commitments to metaphysics, epistemology, morals, and aesthetics have profoundly affected practically every philosophical development that trailed him.

A substantial piece of Kant's work takes up the question "What can we know?" The appropriate response, in the event that it can be expressed merely, is that our insight is restrained to arithmetic and the science of the natural, experimental world. It is impractical, Kant contends, to stretch out learning to the super sensible domain of speculative metaphysics. The reason that information has these limitations, Kant contends, is that the psyche assumes a dynamic part in constituting the characteristics of experience and constraining the mind's accessonly to the empirical domain of room and time.

Kant reacted to his forerunners by contending against the Empiricists that the brain is not a clear slate that is composed upon by the empirical world, and by rejecting the Rationalists 'belief that unadulterated, learning prior knowledge of a mind-free world was conceivable. Reason itself is organized with types of experience and classifications that give a wonderful and intelligent structure to any conceivable protest of empirical experience. These classes cannot be evaded to get at a mind-free world, yet they are vital for experience of spatio-temporal objects with their causal conduct and rational properties. These two theories constitute Kant's well-known transcendental idealism and empirical realism.

John Rawls

John Bordley Rawls (1921–2002) was a standout amongst the most prominent American philosophers after the Second World War. He published his initial book and broadly considered his paramount work, *A Theory of Justice*, only in 1971 when he was 50 years old; however, the book promptly came to be viewed as a standout amongst the most critical works of political philosophy. His philosophy, also termed as Rawlsianism received either strong backing or solid resistance from political philosophers, particularly the proponents of utilitarianism as Rawls's ideas challenge the utilitarian principles.

Rawlsianism

Rawlsianism portrays the notions and perceptions of John Rawls, however most importantly, the term depicts Rawls' principles of justice as he introduced them in his first and most persuasive book, *A Theory of Justice*. In it, he presented the so-called initial position, a hypothetical circumstance including hypothetical subjects who are given the task to create a political and economic structure for a social order in which they are to live in the wake of achieving a consensus. Each of the hypothetical subjects, nevertheless, was put behind the so-called veil of ignorance which denied them of learning about their social position, pay, riches, gender, religion, race and comparative components they could exploit to enhance position for themselves and their close successors. Rawls gave them just the fundamental information about social association and human psychology, and learning of what he called social goods—things each reasonable individual would look for: opportunities, rights, freedoms, riches and confidence. Rawls contended that his hypothetical subjects behind the shroud of numbness would concur on two principals of justice. They would concur that each individual from the general public ought to have (1) political freedom, for example, the freedom of speech, the right to assembly, the right to vote, and so on (equality principle) and that the social and economic imbalances are (2) to the best assistance of the minimum advantaged and (3) to ensure equality of opportunity (difference principle).

Jeremy Bentham

Born on 15 February 1748 in London, England, Jeremy Bentham was quite skilful to be acknowledged as a kid wonder from a very early age. When he was only 3 years of age, Jeremy started perusing a multi-volume history of England and furthermore started studying the Latin dialect. When he was 12, Jeremy was going to Queen's College in Oxford.

Jeremy Bentham is termed as the establishing father of Utilitarianism. In simple definition, Utilitarianism is the philosophy that an ethical act is one which creates the best bliss for the greatest number of individuals. He sketched out this hypothesis in 1789 in his works of the Introduction to the Principles of Morals and Legislation. Bentham started with the basic hypothesis that individuals are inspired by two strong basic desires: (1) To accomplish joy; and (2) To evade grief.

- Bentham's ethical hypothesis was established on the supposition that it is the outcomes of human activities that matter in assessing their genuineness and that the sort of result that matters for human happiness is merely the accomplishment of delight and evasion of pain.
- He contended that the hedonistic value of any human activity is effortlessly computed by considering how seriously its pleasure is felt, to what extent that joy endures, how surely and how rapidly it follows upon the execution of the activity, and how probable it is to produce collateral benefits and maintain a strategic distance from collateral harms. Considering such issues, we arrive at a net estimation of each activity for any person influenced by it.

In essential terms, Bentham's Principle of Utility:

a. Recognizes the basic part of pain and pleasure in human life.
b. Approves or objects to an activity on the basis of the measure of pain or joy achieved,that is, outcomes.
c. Equates good with pleasure and malevolence with pain.
d. Emphasizes that pleasure and pain are equipped for measurement and henceforth measurable.

John Stuart Mill

- Born in London, John Stuart Mill (1806–1873) was the child of James Mill a radical government official, manager and historian of British India. For a period, the Mills leased a house in the grounds of the London home of Jeremy Bentham, the great radical philosopher and establisher of utilitarianism. The young Mill was taught by his father independently from the impact of other youngsters, starting classical Greek at three years of age, trailed by Latin, then history and political economy. In his teenagers, he plainly engaged in radical politics and in his late adolescents, he entered the work of the East India Company in a position comparable to a senior government worker.

Mill was the writer of various expansive and essential books on rationale, political economy and logic, yet his notoriety is to a great extent based on a progression of short essay-length works composed towards the end of his life of which the two most renowned are *Utilitarianism* and *On Liberty*.

Utilitarianism offers an alternative basis to natural law for our moral and political commitments. It affirms that activities, strategies and laws are correct and mandatory in so far as they expand the greatest happiness of the greatest number. Mill comprehends happiness to be the psychological sensation of pleasure and the lack of pain, so he is frequently depicted as a psychological hedonist. Utilitarianism appears to recommend that if a limitation on freedom, (for example, free speech) makes individuals more joyful, then it is acceptable. However, Mill is additionally a protector of unlimited individual freedom. His article, *On Liberty*, is a standout amongst the most critical current safeguards of the freedom of speech, articulation or way of life even when this is offensive to others. Mill's contentions are still conveyed in contemporary open deliberations about multiculturalism and whether the state ought to enact on moral or religious issues.

What propels individuals to do the right thing? Mill asserted universal agreement on the part of moral sanctions in stimulating appropriate behaviourfrom human specialists. However, contrary to Bentham, Mill did not confine himself to the socially enforced external approvals of punishment and reproach, which make the results of inappropriate activity painful. On Mill's opinion, people are also spurred by such internal sanctions as confidence, guilt and conscience. Since we all have social emotions in the interest of others, the unselfish desire for the benefit of all is frequently enough to move us to act ethically. Regardless of the possibility that others don't blame or rebuff me for being in the wrong, I am probably going to censure myself, and that awful emotion is another of the subsequent pains that I sensibly consider when choosing what to do.

"It is better to be a human being dissatisfied than a pig satisfied; better to be Socrates dissatisfied than a fool satisfied. And if the fool, or the pig, is of a different opinion, it is because they only know their own side of the question. The other party to the comparison knows both sides". (Utilitarianism by Mill)

On Liberty

- John Stuart Mill's *On Liberty* is the classic declaration and defence of the view that legislative infringement upon the freedom of individuals is never justified. A truly civil society, he upheld, must continually ensure the civil liberty of its nationals—their safeguard against intervention by an oppressive establishment.

- The oppression of the major population is particularly hazardous to individual freedom, Mill assumed, in light of the fact that the most frequently prescribed cure is to request that the headstrong minority either convince the majority to change its perspectives or figure out how to fit in with socially acknowledged standards.
- The legitimate harmony between individual freedom and legislative establishment, he proposed, can be expressed as a straightforward guideline: "The only purpose for which power can be rightfully exercised over any member of a civilized community, against his will, is to prevent harm to others."
- Although society has a clear obligation for shielding its residents from each other, it should not be meddling with the rest of what they do. Specifically, anything that straightforwardly influences merely the individual resident must remain completely free. No population is really free unless its individual nationals are allowed to take care of themselves.

The Subjection of Women

- One of John Stuart Mill's last and finest scholarly endeavours was composed in backing of a political reason for which he had for some time been a leading champion. *The Subjection of Women* offered both comprehensive argumentation and enthusiastic persuasiveness in intense disapproval to the social and legitimate imbalances ordinarily forced upon women by a male-centric culture.
- Mill brought up, the authority of men over women—like victory or enslavement in some other frame—began in just the brute utilization of physical power. Mill contended that dependence upon physical power and savagery should not be put up with.
- Although it is frequently guaranteed that male authority over women is an entirely normal articulation of natural requirement, Mill discovered minimal bona fide proof for this. Any customary social segregation, made well-known by long understanding and social predominance, will come to appear normal to the individuals who have never mulled over any option. The presence of wilful accommodation by ladies is even more deceptive, on Mill's view, since it could as effortlessly reflect subjugation of psyche and feeling as real emotion.
- Attempts to secure legal rights for women had been a noteworthy issue of Mill's own service in the British Parliament.

Rousseau

Jean-Jacques Rousseau was born on 28 June 1712, in Geneva and died on 2 July 1778 in Ermenonville, France. He was a standout amongst the most essential logicians of the French illumination. He was born in a poor family of a watchmaker. He was not instructed appropriately and obtained casual training by his father at home. At 13-year-old, he worked as an apprentice to an etcher. Nevertheless, Rousseau left Geneva at 16, roaming from place to place, at last moving to Paris in 1742. He made both ends meet during this period working as everything from footman to assistant to an envoy.

Jean-Jacques Rousseau was a French scholar and author of the *Age of Enlightenment*.

Rousseau as a progressive scholar and philosopher starts by scrutinizing the hypothesis of society as the defender and judge of good. One of his fundamental principles is that man is free in the normal state yet that inside society is almost subjugated to that society. He alludes to this liberated individual as the "noble savage" and views him and the characteristic state he lives in as good. On the off chance that there is insidious it is because of the restriction on freedom and to the exploitation of the social reduced.

Rousseau demanded that men must assume the ethical duty regarding the sort of society they build or acknowledge. Obviously, Rousseau utilized men as the comprehensive "humankind", not being banished from sexist dialect amid that time. Both men and women had the ethical duty regarding the general public, on the off chance that they acknowledged what is and it was not great, at that point they bore the obligation regarding it.

In the opinion of Rousseau when man went through the condition of nature, he went from a place where he was consummately allowed to do what he desired to a place where he was restrained by others. In nature, he could opt to construct a house wherever he wished, yet in the public eye he needs to protect it. He should guard it on the grounds that there might be another person who feels that he has a privilege to it. Rousseau was not a supporter of riches, property is fine as everybody has a few and no one has excessive.

Rousseau says that learning comes to a person by nature, man and things. Here he is viewing nature as comparable to gift. Nature is frequently unravelled to the improvement of a kid. The naturalistic chain of importance of learning goals characterizes an entire inversion of conventional reasons for the school, essentially, consummating of man's supreme potential through analysis of literature, philosophy and classics.

Rousseau said that an infant is born great, free from all wrongdoings. After the impact of society he learns malevolence. In Christian period, an infant is born with mortal immorality and accordingly he was dealt with cruelty. Rousseau concentrated on that time of a child where he grows in diverse stages and manufactures his character.

As per Rousseau "Childhood has its place in the sequence of human life; the man must be treated as man and the child as a child". He stressed that a youngster has distinctive limit of learning and he develops his character continuously. He ought to be dealt with otherwise, unlike grown-up people and being a learner he ought to be given sufficient space to learn and develop unaccompanied by others in light of the fact that at last he is the consequence of the social order. Individuals are continually searching for a grown-up in the general public without realizing what a youngster is.

Rousseau was the first to give youth its legitimate place. He felt the need of instruction as indicated by the requests of a kid.

Dalai Lama

The fourteenth Dalai Lama, Tenzin Gyatso, is the other worldly pioneer of Tibet. He was born to a cultivating family on 6 July 1935, in a little village situated in Taktser, Amdo and northeastern Tibet.

Apart from being the profound pioneer of Tibetan Buddhism, His Holiness the fourteenth Dalai Lama has devoted his life to proffering introspective exchanges on the topics of Science and Buddhism, Education and Secular Ethics, Compassion and Universal Responsibility, and in addition Ethics in the fields of Environmental Sustainability, Global Warming and Leadership. He has fairly grasped the quintessence of all religions, as adoring generosity and minding which our twenty-first century society is in much need of. What is more, he has incorporated in his message the importance of all religions, that is, the acknowledgment of the importance of cherishing graciousness and minding, as an advantage to all humankind. In each of these domains, he views people as having basic fundamental esteems, and therefore, he supports that we should cooperate in peace for a superior world. His work in each one of these territories has made him a standout amongst the most powerful figures of the twentieth and twenty-first Centuries.

He has shaped the belief that religion solely is never again satisfactory as a reason for the encouragement of morals, and has turned into a solid voice for the advancement of Secular Ethics, as indicated by the Indian meaning of the words, which is characterized in a more extensive sense as a component of fundamental human moral philosophy, attach importance to all the people including non-devotees, and regarding all religions through veritable and impartial benevolence.

He is a man who lives what he instructs, and his lessons on universal responsibility, morals, sympathy, environmental issues and science of the psyche have turned out to be extraordinary motivation and consolation to a huge number of individuals around the globe. He continually advises us that we are for the most part participating in an extraordinary voyage, so every individual has the ethical duty to make the biological community that is our planet a superior place. Together we bring awesome changes into our reality.

He Advocated the Following Ideals

1. Universal compassion is fundamental to take care of worldwide issues;
2. Compassion is the mainstay of world peace;
3. All world religions are as of now for world peace along these lines, just like all helpful people of whatever belief system;
4. Each individual has an universal obligation to shape organizations to serve human needs.

MORAL THINKERS FROM INDIA

Gautam Buddha

Gautama Buddha, the establisher of Buddhism, was born in an imperial family. He lived for a long time, passing on in 487 B.C. He accomplished edification (i.e., he turned into the Buddha) at the age of thirty-five. Amid the years 532-487 B.C., he systematized the major standards of his idea, which came to be known as Buddhism.

The term Buddha signifies 'illuminated', one who has achieved the information of life. Buddhism originates from the lessons of Siddhartha Gautama, a Hindu sovereign in a little kingdom in South Nepal in the sixth century B.C.

The focal rule of Buddhism is that a specific lifestyle would prompt salvation (nirvana), that is, freedom from the life cycle. Buddhism perceives the four 'noble truths':

1. Life is enduring.
2. The reason for sufferings rests in wants (trishna, lobha), the feelings of connection (moha), and unawareness (avidya).
3. As the wants cause envy, outrage, and disdain, in this manner yielding distress, their disposal is a vital condition for salvation.
4. Therefore, one ought to take after the way prompting the condition of desirelessness, on the grounds that it is the best way to joy (sukh), which is freedom.

Since individuals have wants, they are bound to the wheel of predetermination, and go starting with one body then onto the next, agonizingeach time. Toward the finish of their lives, a great many people have such a large amount of desires left with them that they are born again in another body. They begin the cycle of want and distress afresh.

Keeping in mind the end goal to begin one's excursion along the way of liberation, one ought to follow the Eightfold Path (asthapatha). It comprises right views, right attitude, right speech, right conduct, right means of livelihood, right effort or purpose, right mind control, and right meditation. This way will lead one from the condition of selfishness (ahamkara) to that of compassion (karma). It is by following a path of moral living that one will have the capability to part from the chain of re-birth, adulthood and demise.

Other than the Eightfold Path, one must hold to the accompanying standards:

- Abstain from harming living things.
- Abstain from taking what is not given.
- Abstain from all types of sexual wants (Kama).
- Abstain from all types of lies, that is, lies, in word and deed. Shun common pleasures: no medications, no drink, and no lethargy.

The Buddhist should attempt to raise himself to a condition of brahmavihara, that is, where his body is possessed by divine element. For this he ought to take after four tenets:

- ***Loving kindness (melta)***: A Buddhist secures a total comprehension of his kindred creatures. He sees them as his own particular relatives, whose sufferings he knows.
- ***Compassion (karma)***: Once the Buddhist realizes that he is one of the components in the whole existence, he tries to help other people in their sufferings. He tries to enable them come out of agony.
- ***Joy (mudita)***: The Buddhist shares the delight he gets with each one of the individuals who need it. The Buddha is said to have said over and again: 'Let all be happy.
- ***The condition of being tranquil in mind and temper (upekkha, upeksha)***: Nothing must be permitted to disrupt the clearness of the Buddhist personality. Every robustfeeling is unsafe. Demise does not terrify the individuals who are not attached to life. As such, one who is edified does not fear anybody.

Vardhmana Mahavira

Vardhmana Mahavira, normally viewed as the establisher of Jainism, was born in Vaishali. He achieved pre-eminent learning at the age of forty-two. The valuable period of his religious life might be set in the vicinity of 497 and 467 B.C. However, Jainism asserts to be substantially more ancient than this period. Jains trust that there were twenty-three 'instructors' (tirthankara) before Mahavira, and Mahavira was the last tirthankara.

Buddhism does not recognize the existence of any incomparable god. The notions, in this way, formed around god have no place in it. Neither does it have the possibility of an individual god, one with whom one has relations of adoration and love. In Buddhism, the best way to accomplish salvation (nirvana, i.e., forever liberation from the cycle of birth and demise) is by following an arrangement of ethical and moral principles. It declines to acknowledge the principles of the Hindu social request, that is, the Varna and Jati framework. It does not encourage the arrangement of animal sacrifice.

Jainism likewise comprises of huge numbers of the components that describe Buddhism. It championed the act of 'non-violence' (ahimsa), which is vital to its beliefs.

Swami Vivekananda

Swami Vivekananda is one of the best masterminds of Indian Renaissance. Vivekananda felt sorry on observing the ruined condition of the people.

In the opinion of Swami Vivekananda, social, financial and political recreation of the nation is a pre-essential for the spiritual boost of the people. At the point when the general population request sustenance, to offer religion to a starving people is to affront him. To show religious standards to a starving man is an attack against his confidence. He reprimands unequivocally the failings and shortcomings of the general population, the malicious routine with regards to untouchability, the sentiment of rank predominance, cleric specialty and religious oppression. He wishes to see the general population as affirmed agnostics as opposed to superstitious simpletons, for the sceptics might be of some utilization. In any case, with respect to superstitions it holds away, the cerebrum is bread, the brain is immobilized and debasement immerses life. So it holds good if the humanity ends up plainly agnostic by depending on reason as opposed to aimlessly trusting in two hundred millions of Gods on the influence of anyone.

He has explained dynamic thoughts and intensely contradicted idealist beliefs like supernatural quality. He keeps up that occultism and mysticism have obliterated the general population.

Vivekananda contradicted child marriage, persecution of lower standings, and enslavement of ladies. He focused on the requirement for administration to poor people, ignorant, and the unwell. He trusted that no religion or law was higher than 'service to mankind'. He called his religion *'practical Vedanta'*, in light of the fact that for him, religion must be practiced only. Vivekananda's main goal was to make a 'European society' with India's religion, that is, a religious society where the requirements of all were met. In other words, Vivekananda attempted to consolidate in his contemplations both the spiritual and material perspectives.

Contribution of Swami Vivekananda to India

In many ways, the life and work of Swami Vivekananda denote the ancient procedure of India rediscovering herself in present day times. These are also typical of the courses in which a custom renovates or develops alternative forms of innovation.

As a rule, his commitment to India and to the bigger world might be summed up in four ways:

1. First, in present day India, it was Vivekananda who initially accentuated that our regular day-to-day existences would turn out to be more significant just when spiritualized. It was in this other worldliness that he re-found, in a manner of speaking, India's message to herself and to the world. For Vivekananda, this otherworldly self-acknowledgment prompted individuals to completely understand their own possibilities. Particularly, with regards to a colonized society like that of nineteenth century India, this was commensurate to men and ladies finding more noteworthy self-belief in themselves.
2. Second, despite the fact that the Swami rejected political praxis and West motivated social and religious amendments, his basic message was the strengthening of the general population: through education, aggregate idea and activity yet most importantly, acknowledging the fundamental solidarity of all human presence. In the Hindu convention, austere separation from the world had been disapproved even before Vivekananda. However, it was he who first effectively joined the possibility of individual renunciation to submit social administration. In this sense, he gave new importance or implication to the general thought and establishment of sanyas.

   The Ramakrishna Math and Mission is presently, a working manifestation of this heritage.
3. Third, there is the adoration that Vivekananda reliably showed for the socially underestimated and abused. He could be equally at home in poor homes and royal quarters, be lavishly facilitated by the rich and the influential and furthermore share the coarse chapatti of a scrounger or share the hookah with a shoemaker. It is he, who even before Gandhi, recreated and adequately utilized the more established religious figure of speech of God particularly dwelling in the humble and poor people (daridra narayan).
4. Fourth, it was the Swami's persistent wish to bring back India's pride of place in the gathering of countries, as a civilization which, despite significant historical highs and lows, had yet held hidden strings of commonness and solidarity. In the meantime, similar to his master, Sri Ramakrishna, Vivekananda had complete faith in universality, cosmopolitanism and benevolence. As he saw it, mutual consideration and sympathy amongst human beings was more essential than that originating from a far-off God.

   Notwithstanding above, he additionally took religion not to be some private inclination or eccentricity but rather that which was socially dedicated and accountable. self-determination for him was truly a bigger idea; it had more to do with the liberating of the psyche than the body. The Swami stuck his confidence in people, not establishments and thus picked a way that was noiseless, indirect and natural. One can dare to dream that the all the more persevering facets of his life and work keep on inspiring us in the days to come.

Raja Ram Mohan Roy

The Indian Renaissance of the nineteenth century lays more emphasis basically at restoration of the Indian soul, with the splendour of ancient history and immaculateness significantly influencing religion, society and culture. National arousing has conveyed itself as an impression of religious arousing. In the underlying stages, religious cognizance is observed to be an impression of political awareness. Social and political beliefs, democratic and patriotic yearnings that seek after a superior life have been communicated as religion. The Indian Renaissance started in the nineteenth century by the social reformers does not point towards a total break with religion. It is against the outdated religious traditions and practices from one perspective and reinterpretation and renewal of religion to suit the new conditions on the other.

Macnicol says: *"Raja Ram Mohan Roy is the spiritual father of this Renaissance who appears to be the herald of a new age."*

He is against numerous traditions and convictions of the debauched social framework. He has completely dismissed the code of belief predominant in Hindu society as to their various Gods, ceremonies, the principle of rebirth; embodiments, their routine with regards to idol worship, animal sacrifices and most importantly the detestable routine with regards to sati pervasive in those days which cruelly suppresses.

Keeping in mind the final goal to advance the human uniformity, the expulsion of the handicaps of ladies in social life is another vital issue. He supported the conceding of equal property rights to men and ladies. He battles in help of widow remarriage and against youngster marriages. He promotes education for women. He looks to embrace the new esteems introduced by Western science to merge them with the conventional estimations of India to address the difficulty of the new age.

Hinduism as he comprehends is established in a wide humanistic standpoint. In this way, he has set himself the undertaking of cleaning Hinduism and clearing the sluggishness of superstitions which have built upthrough the ages. He is of the sentiment that the renaissance of Hinduism as a genuine national religion would suit to the new states of social life. His humanism can be called as universal humanism for his accentuation on world cooperation with a liberal soul, and for his laying emphasis on warm relationship among the different countries of the world.

Mohandas Karamchand Gandhi

Mohandas Karamchand Gandhi was one of the not very many individuals who presented a thought for a historic period. That thought was practice of non-violence. Gandhi's ideology of non-violence demanded that individuals' battle for their rights ought to never defy their fundamental commitment to regard life.

Gandhi was both religious and liberal, and saw all religions as ways to achieve a similar objective. He was enlivened by the lessons of Jesus, specifically, the accentuation on affection for everybody, even one's adversaries, and the need to exert oneself for justice. He likewise took from Hinduism the significance of activity in one's life, without worry for progress. The Hindu content Bhagavad-Gita expresses:

"On action alone be thy interest/Never on its fruits/Abiding in discipline perform actions/ Abandoning attachment/Being indifferent to success or failure".

Gandhi's way to deal with the truth is religious as opposed to philosophical. He moved toward reality through non-violence.

Non-violence is a vital fragment of each religion. He says that: 'Non-violence is in Hinduism, it is in Christianity as well as in Islam. If non-violence disappears, Hindu Dharma disappears. Islam does not forbid its followers from following non-violence as a policy.'

In the wake of having examined the Bhagavad-Gita against the foundation of Indian culture and convention, he has arrived at the conclusion that the crucial teaching of the Gita is to take after truth and non-violence.

Gandhi's commitment to the human development lies in his showing truth and peacefulness in each stroll of life for people or countries.

As indicated by him peacefulness is the kingdom of heaven. It guarantees peace and euphoria, amicability and harmony, sensitivity and co-operation, in human issues. These are its natural products. As the competitor looks for the kingdom of paradise as the most astounding objective, so peacefulness is the Heaven, it is a flawless state.

Gandhi as a Practical Idealist

Gandhi was not a visionary but rather he guaranteed to be a pragmatic dreamer. He was a man of activity. It was the optimist that influenced him to work as a useful man. He was additionally an irrepressible positive thinker. His idealism depended on the conviction that man is enriched with unending conceivable outcomes of improvement. His faith in the law as the perfect is undisputable. It makes a difference whether people miss the mark regarding the perfect. In spite of the fact that he knew about the truth, his endeavouring was continuously to conform to the belief.

It is a wayof centring his devotion to the definitive objective. He needs to tread the correct way without diversion. This is the benchmark by which man's advance is measured. Gandhi's theory was the immediate aftereffect of human relations and it was in the circle of human collaboration that his policy took solid shape. His methodology was progressive and human. The world is there for every realistic reason. It is the field of most noteworthy action.

Gandhi has confidence in the imperfect man who can enhance his condition by developing an impeccably blameless heart unequipped for malevolence. Subsequently, the error-prone man, being an obstruction to his own self-improvement, can be redressed to take after the way of advance in good spirit. It can just occur through life-lessons. Gandhi states that: "It is not literacy or learning which makes a man but education for real life."

Sarvepalli Radhakrishnan

Among present-day Indian scholars, Radhakrishnan was an extraordinary mastermind who was a professor in Eastern and Western colleges and furthermore as a Vice-Chancellor. As the leader of the University Education Commission he had an event to test profound into the issues of advanced education in India. Alongside his varied experience of the field of education, Radhakrishnan had wide learning and profound knowledge into Indian and Western, old and contemporary way of life. He was without a doubt a standout amongst the most qualified people to talk about Indian philosophy of education with the administration. His perspectives are discovered scattered in his different books, for example, *An Idealist View of Life, The Philosophy of Rabindranath Tagore, The Brahma Sutra, The Bhagavad-Gita, The Hindu View of Life, Eastern Religion and Western Thought.*

Radhakrishnan was a promoter of antiquated Indian Vedanta philosophy. He was a perfectionist scholar. He characterized philosophy as a mix of reflection and instinct. Radhakrishnan's objective of philosophy is to explore that amalgamation which may incorporate every facets of creation. Philosophy in his opinion: *"Is an attempt of human being to know the problems of creation and the nature of ultimate reality."*

Radhakrishnan conceded the value of reason and confidence, rationale and encounter and the value of perceptual, theoretical and instinctive knowledge in education. As per him, instinctive knowledge is the most elevated learning and is an indispensable experience. He clarified spiritualist experience as a piece of instinctive experience. Overall experience is picked up by total self and it is substantially higher than some other experience picked up by add up to self and it is considerably higher than some other experience gained by total self and innovative understanding has an imperative place in all-out information. His reasoning has been properly translated as essential experience, and this experience discovers place for each other kind of experience in it.

As indicated by Radhakrishnan, human identity is not controlled by monetary or physical condition. So far as physical changes are concerned they might be by and large dictated by the environment by the human will which is allowed to choose to win or lose. The genuine human liberty is the liberty of wish. In the custom of antiquated Indian scholars Radhakrishnan had conceded the principle of Karma. As indicated by this standard our present is controlled by our past and future relies on the present. In the expressions of Radhakrishnan:

"Karma or relationships with the past does not mean that man cannot do anything freely but free action is involved in it."

The law of Karma is not fatalism "An individual will gain according to the use of his energy. The world will respond to the individual Jivatma's demand. The nature will reply the insistent call of the man."

Similar to Karl Marx, Radhakrishnan trusted that man can transform the world. On the premise of his determination he can build his future. The standards of Nature are the standards of impartiality. In nature and in human world, all over, one all-inclusive celestial law functions. Along these lines, the law of Karma is not an outer yet an inner determinant of human life. In the line of assessment, man is differentiated by self-awareness which is not discovered either in plants or in creatures. The mental procedures cannot be translated with regard to physical changes. The physical developments do not clarify total conduct.

❑❑❑

Concerns and Dilemmas Related to Ethics in Government Institutions

4 CHAPTER

DEFINITION AND SIGNIFICANCE OF ETHICS

Ethics has been recognized as the 'Science of morals; the rules of conduct, the science of human duty' since the seventeenth century. Hence, in common terms, ethics can be defined as the principles that influence a person's or a group's behaviour according to both the science of the good and the nature of the right. Mention of the ethical concerns of governance can be abundantly found in Indian scriptures and other treatises such as *Ramayana*, *Mahabharata*, *Bhagvad Gita*, *Buddha Charita*, *Arthashastra*, *Panchatantra*, *Manusmriti*, *Kural*, *Shukra Niti*, *Kadambari*, *Raja Tarangani* and *Hitopadesh*. At the same time, one can also refer to the views provided by the Chinese philosophers such as Lao Tse, Confucius and Mencius related to ethical governance. Western philosophy refers to three eminent schools of ethics. The first, motivated by Aristotle, states that qualities (such as justice, charity and generosity) are dispositions to act in ways that turn out to be beneficial for the one who holds these virtues and the society of which he is a part. The second, inspired by Immanuel Kant, holds that the concept of duty is important for morality: human beings are destined, as per the knowledge of their duty as rational beings, to follow the categorical rule to respect others with whom they interact. The third includes the Utilitarian viewpoint that states that the guiding principle of conduct should make large number of people happier. There are ample of ethical guidelines for rulers as per western thoughts, whether in a monarchy or a democracy. Mention of these guidelines can be traced in the works of Plato, Aristotle, Thomas Jefferson, Alexander Hamilton, Thomas Penn, John Stuart Mill, Edmund Burke and others.

The theory of justice given by Rawls deals with the adaptation of two fundamental principles of justice, which will guarantee a just and morally acceptable society in return.

- The former principle assures each person a right to have the most extensive basic liberty compatible with liberty of others.
- The latter principle holds that social and economic positions should be open for all and advantageous to everyone.

The aim of Rawls here is to make sure to depict how such principles would be globally accepted. Here, his composition states only general ethical issues. He presents a hypothetical 'veil of ignorance', where all 'players' in the social game would be positioned in a situation called the 'original position'. With only a general knowledge about the realities of 'life and society', 'rationally' sensible choice should be made by each player regarding the type of social institution they would enter into contract with. Denying the players any specific information about themselves compels them to embrace a generalized point of view that that is similar to the moral point of view to a great extent. This viewpoint, which is mainly related to moral conclusions, can be formed without rejecting the prudential viewpoint and posting a moral outlook just by following one's own prudential reasoning under any procedural bargaining.

Wisdom on administrative ethics means that in Administrative State, the public administrators are regarded as the 'guardians'. Hence, it is expected that they should respect public trust and not violate it. Two crucial questions that emerged in this context are 'why guardians should be guarded?' and 'Who guards the guardian?' It is important to guard administrators against their bent to misinterpret public interest, encourage self-interest, practice corruption and cause subversion of national interest. They are also required to be guarded by the external establishments such as the judiciary, legislature, political executive, media and civil society establishments. These different ways of control turn out to be instruments of accountability.

EVOLUTION OF ETHICAL CONCERNS IN ADMINISTRATION

It is of utmost importance to acknowledge that Political Science and the science of Management have largely influenced the discipline of Public Administration in the initial years of its growth. On the one hand, the philosophical ideals of Public Administration were influenced primarily by Political Science. On the other hand, Management Sciences designed its technological aspect. The early Political Science was a mix of Moral Philosophy and Political Economy, whereas its current curriculum includes secular, practical, empirical and scientific aspects relate to the past century. During the initial years of the last century, Political Science students in the USA were discouraged due to lack of the ethical approach in the Gilded Age. Influenced by the interaction with the German universities and by the thinking of scholars such as J.N. Burgess, E.J. James, A.B Hart, A.L Lovell and F.J Goodnow, they thought of recreate Political Science as a true science. They increasing started to observe and analyse 'actual governments'. Natural and Social Sciences have had a great influence on their ideas and approaches.

Later, scholars such as Herbert Simon were influenced by the logical positivism of the Austrian School, resulting in the increase in followers with the common aim of developing a Science of Politics and a Science of Administration that will likely `predict and control' political and administrative life. As Dwight Waldo comments, there was a shift from the old faith that good government was the government of moral men to a morality that was unrelated and that suitable institutions and expert personnel were the deciding factors in shaping good government. `The new amorality became almost a request for professional respect'.

Due to the prominence of behaviouralism until the mid-1960s, the ethical issues in the study of Political Science and Public Administration were marginalized further. Beginning of Post-behaviouralism in Political Science and of the accent on New Public Administration in Public Administration helped scientific methods of Behaviouralim and humanistic (read `ethical') values to strike a balance with administration, resulting in resolving the dispute between facts and values.

The present form of public administration focuses mainly on the `values' of equity, justice, humanism, human rights, gender equality and compassion. The movement of Good Governance, started by the World Bank in 1992, emphasizes, *inter alia*, on the ethical and moral conduct of administrators. Although the New Public Management movement focuses on administrative effectiveness, administrative ethics in its broader manifestation take the centre stage in the New Public Administration. Both the movements are complementary to each other.

The ideal-type structure of bureaucracy, coined by Max Weber, also stated on an ethical imperative of bureaucratic behaviour. Weber (1947) observed:

'In the rational type, it is a matter of principle that the members of the administrative staff should be completely separated from ownership of the means of production and administration. Officials, employees and workers attached to the administrative staff do not themselves own the non-human means of production and administration.... These exist, furthermore, in principle complete separation of property belonging to the organization, which is controlled within the sphere of office and the personal property of the official, which is available for his own private uses'.

Weber's study reveals that there is a need to avoid misuse of an official position for personal gains. While his ideal-type structure related to bureaucracy is not empirical, yet it has an empirical flavour, because it seems to have considered the existential reality of bureaucratic behaviour. Message, donot misuse official property for personal benefit, is also clear from a normative angle even after knowing that Weber was not normative in his ideal-type constructs.

Bureaucrats have been criticized by most of the critics of real-world bureaucracies, including Harold Laski, Carl Friedrich, Victor Thompson and Warren Bennis, for flouting the specified rules of moral conduct. Fred Riggs, while debating the qualities of a prismatic society like **`formalism'** and **'nepotism'**, highlights the wide gap between the **`ideal'** and the **`real'** in administrative behaviour. It is difficult to let these deviations go as they are too glaring. Immoral behaviour thus came out as an integral element of **`bureau pathology'**.

CONTEXT OF ETHICS AND ITS SIGNIFICANCE FOR PUBLIC ADMINISTRATION

Ethics, keeping in view an entire society or a social sub-system, develops over a long period of time and is affected, while nurturing and growing, by various environmental factors. Administrative ethics is no way different. It is the creation of several contextual structures and always keeps on growing and changing. Some of these contextual factors that affect ethics in the public administrative systems are as follows:

The Historical Context

The history of a country greatly shapes the ethical character of the governance system. During the early phase of the America, the ethical setting of the American Public Administration was destroyed by the Spoils System in the USA. The then American President Jackson asserted 'To victor belong the spoils'. If President Garfield was not assassinated by a disgruntled job seeker in 1881, things would have continued the same way. It is only after Garfield's assassination that civil service reforms took place in the USA. The constitution of Civil Service Commission in 1883 was the first important step in this direction.

Indian governance system has long been plagued with unethical practices. Some of the corrupt practices practised by the administrators of those times are mentioned in Kautilya's *Arthashastra*. Corruption also existed in the Mughal Empire and the Indian princely states, where courtiers and administrative functionaries used 'bakashish' for selling and buying favours. Even the East India Company was not immune to corruption and corrupt people who were criticized even by the British parliamentarians.

The existence of forces of probity and immorality together can be traced back to ancient times. The intensity of these forces depends upon the support these attain from the main actors of politico-administrative system. More worrisome aspect of it is that a long heritage of immoral practices in governance is likely to grow the tolerance level for administrative immorality. In most developing countries with a colonial history, the gap between the people and the government continues to be wide. During the colonial era, a majority of people do not happily accept the lawfulness of governance and hence true devotion to the rulers was a rare phenomenon. As the differences between the governing elite and the citizens have been reduced significantly in the new democratic regimes, affinity and trust between them has not achieved the desired result. Regrettably, the rulers do not seem to have embraced the essence of emotional unity with the citizens. The heritage of competitive collaboration between the people and the administrators remains. This relationship adversely affected 'administrative ethics'.

The Socio-cultural Context

The nature of governance system is determined by values that infuse the social order in a society determine. The Indian society today had more love for wealth compared to any other value. The means-ends debate has been put on the backseat while busy in generating wealth. Unfortunately, ends have gained supremacy over means. Hunt for wealth in itself is not bad. In fact, it is a mark of civilizational progress. What is more important is the means used while being engaged in this hunt.

We appear to be living in an economic or commercial society, where unit-dimensional growth of individuals is preferred and valued, where ends have been overshadowed by means, and ideals have been inundated under the weight of more practical concerns of economic progress. Can we change this social order? Mahatma Gandhi was very much eager to transform the priority-order of the Indian society, but rarely anyone supported his radical thinking that was immersed in a strong moral order. This is a fact that after

Gandhi, no one has ever matched his persona and there has been not a single strong voice in independent India challenging the authority of 'teleology and unidimensionalism'. It is sad that our families and educational system have failed as a whole as no one has questioned this unilinear growth of society and no serious steps have been initiated to inject morality into the impressionable minds of our youth. We have baldly failed on these fronts. There is a need to devise new viewpoints on what kind of the Indians we wish to evolve and how? Till then, it is important to focus on the non-social fronts.

It is not confirmed whether the matters of morality are embedded in the religious ethos of a society. Wealth earned through illegal or wrong means is not taken in a good taste as per the Indian religious scriptures. Amusingly, Thiru Valluvar's *Kural*, written two thousand years ago in Tamil Nadu, states that although wealth is akin to fame, respect and a chance to aid and serve others, but the same should be attained by right means only. Is this dictum capable to form the basis of our socio-moral orientation?

A class of people believes that integrity among Protestants and Parsees is relatively higher in contrast to other religions, and one can easily trace the roots of such integrity in the well-ingrained customs of these religions. However, this view does not fit for all, as there exist other religious and secular groups eminent for their high moral conduct. The cultural system of any nation, with its religious orientation, plays a big part in framing the work ethics of its people. For example, it is only because of importance given to hard work, feature of the Protestant ethics, that several Christian societies have been able to boost their per capita productivity. Although physical labour is considered good by Judaism, the Hindu and Islamic societies consider physical labour to be inferior to the mental work.

It is not sure whether work ethics are linked with religious moorings. Although subjective aspects, they make for an exciting study. The family system and the educational system make powerful tools of socialization and training of the mind in its early years. It is evident that if good values are inculcated in schools in early years, it will likely have a good and positive impact on society.

Legal-judicial Context

Nation's legal system is credited with the responsibility to ensure the effectiveness of the ethical concerns in governance system. It is very important to frame efficient and well-formulate laws, keeping in mind fair and honest conduct, to distinguish chaff from grain in the ethical universe. Conversely, nebulous laws, which are not formulated in an efficient manner and have vague explanations about corruption, will only help violators to conduct more of these acts as it would not be able to instil the fear of God or fear of law among them. Therefore, efficient judiciary with fast-tract justice system is necessary to curtail immorality in public affairs. In contrast, a slow-moving judiciary will only help perpetrators of crimes to remain fearless by giving them freedom through prolonged trials and benefits of doubt.

In the same way, the anti-corruption wing of the government, through its complex procedures, unintentionally provide relief to the accused who are indirectly helped by slow and tricky procedures. In India, there is a dearth of effective anti-corruption institution. As already read in Unit 7 earlier on in this Course, the Lok Pal is still in the process of finalization, Lok Ayuktas are weak and ineffective agencies, while the state vigilance bodies are low-key actors. The concerns are too obvious to give any explanation.

The Political Context

The political leadership, either in power or outside power, leaves significant impact on the customs and values of citizens. The rulers do rule the minds, but in particularly a democratic setup, all political parties, pressure groups and the media play a big role in moulding attitudes on moral questions. If politicians act with full ethics and morality, as can be seen in the Scandinavian countries and in most South Asian countries, political morality can be attained by the administrative system very easily.

The Indian election system is regarded to be the biggest catalyst for political corruption. Elected candidates likely earn money spent during elections through fair or foul means. Although fair has limits, foul has none. As it is evident that the administrative class–civil servants at higher, middle as well as lower levels – belongs to society itself, they are likely to work as keeping in mind the customs, values and behavioural patterns predominant in the society. It is impractical to think that the administrators will be insulated from the orientations and norms present in the society.

Although the argument, presented here, has a valid point, there can be a disagreement that the rulers are expected to have stronger moral fibre than the subjects. Due to the lack of any means to protect and nurture administrative morality vis-à-vis the general social morality, such a belief remains an elusive ideal. Hence, it is of utmost importance to mine the problem further.

In India, the actions of civil servants are largely influenced by the politicians. Political class has an upper hand over civil servants. It is sad that moral codes in a nation like India are influenced more by its politicians as compared to any other social group. Objective and honest media can play a good role in curtailing the evil of corruption. It may also encourage administrators to embrace ethical behaviour. Hence, those who control the media should act with responsibility to curtail evil practices. The efforts in this direction are underway as many channels have been regularly airing their 'expose' on malpractices in the system. This role of the media, sans sensationalism, will play a great role in making India a better place to live.

The Economic Context

There exists a positive correlation between level of economic development of a nation and the level of ethics in the governance system. Even when there is no causal relation between the two, a correlation cannot be ruled out. Low level of economic development along with inequalities in the economic order is expected to form a gap among social classes and groups. Class belonging to deprived society will likely be attracted to indulge in unfair means to fulfil their needs. It is evident that rich will mainly be more honest (though they can afford to be so) as compared to the poor who are more likely to compromise with the principles of integrity.

After the introduction of liberalized economic regime in developing nations, the WTO regime stressed on following the rules of integrity in industry, trade, management and the governance system. This is what Fred Riggs would call `exogenous' inducements to administrative change.

ISSUE OF ETHICS: FOCI AND CONCERNS

Now, the moral obligation of an administrative system gives rise to an important question. Is the administrative system restricted to acting morally in its conduct or does it also share the duty of shielding and encouraging an ethical order in the larger society? Although there is a focus on the aspect of probity within the administrative system under the administrative morality, for nurturing and protecting the basic moral values, it is important to keep in mind the aspect of the responsibility of the governance system (of which the administrative system is an integral part) to frame and sustain an ethical atmosphere in the socio-economic system. As per the moral political philosophy, the rulers will not only be moral themselves, but would also be the protectors of morality in a society. Truly, it is required by a person to be moral for being a guardian of wider morality. Both the obligations are knotted.

It is known that ethical decision-making is the main step in attaining administrative morality. It is almost impossible to separate ethical decision-making from the questions of facts and values, resulting in integrating the science of administration with the ethics of administration. In this integrated system, empirical concern that values the normative concerns in the distribution of administrative services is valued.

Which are the important apprehensions related to administrative ethics? There are a number of values regarded necessary in an administrative action. Nevertheless, one has to pick most important values in being selective. It is now time to focus on values of justice, fairness and objectivity. Woodrow Wilson, 'The Study of Administration' (1887), in his first speech stated that justice was more important than sympathy, thus putting justice at the first position in value-hierarchy in a governance system. Paradoxically, despite discussing the formal-legal aspects of administrative law since then, very little analysis has been done on the philosophical dimension of administrative justice.

Other integral parts of administrative justice include fairness and objectivity, i.e., other two issues of ethical decision-making. When administrators act wisely and honestly, they are thought of as impartial and fair and not get attracted by nepotism, favouritism and greed while making decisions of governance. Objectivity should not be misinterpreted as a mechanical and firm adherence to laws and rules. When seen from the point of view related to decision-making, it has certainly broader consequences surrounding a set of positive orientations.

In the present times, the scope of ethics has expanded itself to involve all major realms of human existence. Here are certain salient aspects of ethics in public administration. Largely, they could be defined as following maxims:

- *Maxim of Legality and Rationality*: An administrator will abide by the codes and conduct devised to administer and direct several categories of policies and decisions.

- ***Maxim of Responsibility and Accountability***: An administrator would not think twice in taking responsibility for his judgement and actions. Moreover, he would be eager to be held responsible to superior authorities of governance and even to the people who are the real beneficiaries of his decisions and actions.
- ***Maxim of Work Commitment***: An administrator would be dedicated to his obligations and accomplish his duties with involvement, intelligence and dexterity. As Swami Vivekananda observed: 'Every duty is holy and devotion to duty is the highest form of worship'. This would also let them learn respect for time, punctuality and fulfilment of promises made. Work is regarded not as a burden but as a chance to serve and fruitfully contribute to society.
- ***Maxim of Excellence***: An administrator would work to maintain the highest level of quality in administrative judgements and action and would not side line standards because of convenience or complacency. In a competitive international environment, an administrative system should devotedly follow the fundamentals of Total Quality Management.
- ***Maxim of Fusion***: An administrator would wisely bring together individual, organizational and social goals to devise unison of ideals and inculcate commitment in his behaviour for such a fusion. Concerning conflicting aims, a concern for ethics should decide the choices made.
- ***Maxim of Responsiveness and Resilience***: An administrator will react successfully to the appeals and challenges from the external and internal environment. By adapting to environmental transformation, he keeps the ethical norms of conduct. When deviation from the set ethical norms is noticed, the administrative system would show flexibility and bounce back into the established ethical mould at the earliest chance.
- ***Maxim of Utilitarianism***: While framing and executing policies and judgements, an administrator will make it a point that the benefits lead to the greatest good (happiness, benefits) of the greatest number.
- ***Maxim of Compassion***: Without flouting the prescribed codes and conduct, an administrator would show compassion for the poor, the disabled and the weak while making judgements. At least, it is important for him to be impartial and not shown any favouritism to any section of the society.
- ***Maxim of Transparency***: An administrator will decide on and execute policies in a transparent way so that those influenced by the decisions and who wish to estimate their rationale, will be able to recognize the reasons for such decisions and the sources of information on which these decisions were made.

There are still many doctrines those could be added to the above list of maxims of morality in administration. However, the overall goal is to guarantee 'Good Governance' keeping in mind ethical principles, practices, orientations and behaviour. There are no doctrines involved in the process of describing administrative ethics. It is important to keep in mind the positive significance of administrative action and not just seemingly normal modes of administrative processes. Some of the important concerns and foci of ethics are described as follows.

ETHICAL DILEMMAS

The new century appears to have started with the pressure regarding ethical and philosophical dilemmas which leave experts and academics of public administration alike in a fix. Only answers and convictions were predominant at the dawn of the 20th century, this century is facing new questions, uncertainties and doubts arising as a result of the overarching procedure of the globalization of market economies and IT as well as the localization of political struggle, authority systems and culture. The process called the institutionalization of doubt (Giddens, 1990) then has a wider significance.

Dealing with Ethical Dilemmas in Public Administration

In a situation full of uncertainties and faced with the fundamental question what to do and how to act in difficult times, and to the level that contrasted values or decisional premises could be used in the situation, one is standing in front of the world of ethical dilemmas or that of 'hard choices'.

Dilemma has a wider scope as compared to a problem, irrespective of the difficulty or complexity of the latter (Rapoport, 1960). It is because of the reason that it is almost impossible to solve dilemma, unlike problem, in the terms in which they are firstly catered to decision-maker. When facing a dilemma, the decision-makers are not only tackling opposed and perhaps equally unwelcome options. They are facing a challenge in which one can only be satisfied by sacrificing other. It can then be said that deciphering a dilemma is akin to a zero sum game, in which the choice of one value alternative is certainly followed by the annulment of the other. Therefore, this way of solving the dilemma would be an ambiguity in terms and a misnomer as the resolution reached likewise would appear to be only a scission and a dichotomic split of the intertwined aspects of the issue at hand.

A more effective and efficient way of dealing with the dilemma is by altering the terms of reference and reframing the whole situation, which will then be considered and arranged among themselves in a more systematic and coherent manner. Naturally, dilemmas are seen to be thriving in complex establishments, which lack the expertise to tackle them effectively. As a result, state officials and civil servants facing serious dilemmas find it difficult to find any solution and slip into the state of confusion and embarrassment. These situations force public administration into a state of confusion and indeterminacyinstead of working as a well-organized state of legitimate purposes. In hard case, ethical ambiguity and dearth of clarity about overall values to act may come close to set free a spirit of unbound relativism if not cynicism whereby everything stands. In a situation where everything stands and anything goes, there is nothing left that can be taken seriously, neither ethics and values nor rights and responsibilities of public servants and citizens alike.

In order to understand the host of norms that enter and frequent the organizational landscape of public administration in different ways, a number of ground rules have been recognized which, first, define basic administrative dilemmas in an organized form, and second, are needed to be kept in mind while being engaged in the business of dealing with them. It is likely that the host of guiding ethical doctrines, heuristic in nature, is built based on an ideal type (after Max Weber, 1964, 1978). To make sequential mode of their application in concrete cases manifest, the values have also been set in the form of a lexical ordering and a kind of scalar logic (after John Rawls, 1971).

The advanced list of fundamental principles or criteria that helps in integrating and rearranging the procedure of tackling ethical dilemmas in public administration includes following: (1) democratic liability of administration, (2) the rule of law and the law of legality, (3) professional reliability and (4) openness to civil society.

TOWARDS NEW DIMENSIONS OF ETHICS

The best way to ensure best standards of administrative ethics includes promoting 'sunshine' in public administration. Openness is seen as the foe of corruption. Freedom of Information or Right to Information Acts have been practised in almost all countries of the world. Freedom of information and open hearing provisions have been a vital part of the Administrative Procedure Act at the federal level in the USA. Indian government amended the Freedom of Information Act of 2002 as Right to Information Act, enacted in 2005. In addition, lots of states like Goa, Rajasthan, Tamil Nadu and Maharashtra have framed and implemented laws that help in setting accountability of public employees through this device.

It is to be understood that just framing of legislation alone is not enough, its implementation would need a will of the State, willingness of administrators and an initiative along with courage on the part of citizens themselves. The State machinery should always be upfront in dealing with the officials obstructing the smooth execution of Right to Information Act. The contemporary views of regarding every information as `secret' must be shunned and all should strive for greater openness and transparency. This effort will only be successful if change of mind-set happens of administrators to change the thinking of administration at all levels, more particularly at the cutting-edge level.

The movement to seek transparency will fail without the active participation and demand for the fructification of this Right. Although enactment of this act has given some hope for the bright future, there are still serious efforts to be made for ensuring its effective implementation. People's groups, such as the one led by Aruna Roy, will have to continue to take initiative on a massive scale. Even the educational system and the media will need to play a purposive role in this realm.

In the USA, 'whistle blowing' is a way to lodge their (public employees) protest against any activity that is illegal or immoral. This is considered as moral and appropriate, and legitimate and statutorily protected. They can even resign from their post to give more fire to their actions.

The USA has a hotline, called `Fraud Net', for reporting any case of fraud, waste and abuse. This paves the way for any employee, who witnessed any act of misconduct, anonymously report such instances for investigation to the General Accounting Office. In addition, the American public employees have Constitutional protection on addressing matters of public concern like dangers to public health or safety.

Britain also took some steps to ensure control of illegal activities by enacting a new appeals procedure for civil servants. This procedure lets a civil servant to raise concerns, confidentially, with an individual outside his normal hierarchy. If he thinks response as unsatisfactory or unreasonable, he has the right to report the matter to the Civil Service Commissioner. The Constitutional Review Commission in India discussed the viability of whistleblowing, but the same was not accepted as a viable choice. This is the right time to have a fresh perspective on this issue.

❑❑❑

Case Studies

5 CHAPTER

UNDERSTANDING CASE STUDY

A case study is the explanation of an administrative circumstance or a typical life situation that involves decision making or problem solving. It could be an actual scenario that really happened just as mentioned, or a hypothetical scenario. Most case studies are composed in such a manner that the reader acts as administrator whose duty is to decide to help solve the problem. The case study model as a learning mechanism has seen a surge in its use in recent times globally. The Harvard Business School is credited with developing the case-study approach. It is thought of as a better form of elucidating the concepts to students. Mainly concerned with the administrator and the business managers, the case-study model is of great help as the administrator/manager often finds himself in dilemma conditions while tackling day-to-day management issues. The case studies let an individual to comprehend the condition better and put himself in the shoe of the person who has to take the decision. Hence, it prepares the candidate for various decision-making circumstances in the career. In reality, case study examination lets candidates to attain following two skills:

- *Applying theories to real situations*
- *Generating solutions to real problems*

The UPSC has also recently included in its curriculum the case-study model in scrutinizing the civil service aspirants.

TACTICS TO ANSWER CASE-STUDY QUESTIONS

UPSC had given three model case studies for the Main Examination 2013. These studies were analysed as below:

- *Real-life situations*
- *Administrative situations*

Principally, the UPSC desires to scan the aspirants on the following qualities:

- *Ability to deal with the ethical dilemmas in real life situations.*
- *Ability to deal with the ethical dilemmas in administrative situations.*
- *Administrative aptitude to deal with complex management issues.*

These problems are subjective, and there is no 'One-Best-Answer'. In particularly the mains examination, the way we take a decision making stage is more important. These case study problems can be solved in the following four steps. It is okay to use concepts or theory or quotes, but be careful not to overemphasize on this aspect.

The Four Step Process

- Identify the problem/issue
- Analyse the problem/dilemmas
- Identify the decision choices available
- Make the decision with reason

Starting with the Main Examination 2013, the UPSC started supplying Question-cum-Answer sheets. The space for answers has been fixed, and the aspirants are bound to answer within the space. So it becomes essential for all to decide what to write and till what extent. The four-step process helps in analysing and taking a decision. The definite solution in the examination need not be the whole analysis, it can just be the decision and the reasons.

SAMPLE CASE STUDY

You have been working with your team for almost a year. One of your subordinates Mr. A is very effective and hardworking; he takes responsibility and gets things done. However, you have heard that, that Mr. A makes loose comments about women. Mrs. X who is working under Mr. A comes to you, she is visibly disturbed. She tells you that Mr. A has been making undue advances towards her and had even asked her to go out for dinner with him. She wants to give a written complaint seeking action against Mr. A. What would you do and why?

Step-1: *Issue—Sexual harassment in office.*

Step-2: *Dilemma—The sexual harassment complaint is against a 'very effective and hardworking' subordinate. Should you take strict action or lenient view? You have already heard about such behaviour of this subordinate. So there must be some background to the allegations being made by Mrs. X.*

Step-3: *Taking action against Mr. A means demotivation of Mr. A due to disciplinary action, leading to problems in executing the projects in the office.*

1. *Not taking action leads to more such cases, indiscipline and other serious administrative issues.*
2. *What is more important—moral stand or administrative expediency?*

Step-4: *Sexual harassment in office is an unacceptable behaviour and has to be punished. Mrs. X wants to give the complaint in writing. The procedures have to be followed in such cases. The Supreme Court in Visakha case (1997) has given guidelines for action in case of sexual harassment at work places.*

- *The written complaint of Mrs. X will be sent to the Complaint Committee (Every office is supposed to have a committee to deal with such sexual harassment complaints).*
- *On the basis of the enquiry report of the Complaints Committee, criminal proceedings will be initiated in case of violations of any provisions of the Indian Penal Code.*

The answer need not be in the step process. The above four steps are to be used to take a decision. The solution should just explain—'What would you do and why?'—The decision/course of action and reasons. Since the question is 'What would you do....', so write the answer in first person. 'I will send the complaint to Complaints Committee...'.

SAMPLE CASE STUDY

You have grown up with X, who has been your best friend since childhood. You have shared your joys and sorrows and have been each other's confidante. Both of you are in your final year graduation and writing your final exams. In the exam, you notice that your friend is copying and cheating a lot. What would you do and why?

Step-1: *Issue—Cheating in exam.*

Step-2: *Dilemma—The person cheating is your best friend.*

It is immoral to cheat in exam. But complaining to the examiner will destroy the career of your friend.

Step-3: *The options before you are*

1. *Be silent—which is immoral on your part.*
2. *Complaint to the examiner—Your friend might get debarred from examination and his entire career is at stake. After complaining, you might get disturbed yourself and hence, you might spoil your performance in the exam.*
3. *Tell friend not to copy.*

Step-4: *Will adopt the following course of action:-*

- *Indicate to the friend not to copy otherwise you will complain to the examiner.*
- *If he stills copies, tell loudly to the examiner that someone in the room is copying but you can't name them. (This will make the friend alert and knows that you are serious about it).*
- *Still continues copying, complain to the examiner.*
- *The above course will take care of your moral conscience and the fact that you have given a chance to your friend to reform without causing irreparable damages. However, if situation compels, you will take the necessary strong action.*
- *(There are no correct answers in such questions. You may or may not agree with the answer given above).*

SAMPLE CASE STUDY

You are posted as the Medical Superintendent of a District-level Govt. Hospital which caters to the need of poor patients from surrounding rural areas along with the local people from the district town. As such the hospital has very good infrastructure and adequate equipment to cater to this need. It also receives sufficient funds to meet the recurring expenditure. In spite of this, there have been repeated complaints particularly from the patients which include the following

(i) Very poor maintenance and unhygienic conditions in hospital premises.

(ii) The hospital staff frequently demanding bribes from the patients for the services rendered.

(iii) The negligent attitude of the Doctors resulting in times of causalities.
(iv) Siphoning of a substantial stock of medicine by the staff and selling it out.
(v) Strong nexus between the senior Doctors of the hospital and the owners of the local private nursing homes and testing labs as a result of which the patients are strongly misled and dissuaded from availing the hospital facilities and rather compelled to purchase costly medicine from market and get medical tests and even operations done from private medical houses.
(vi) There also exist a notorious employee union which puts undue pressure and resents any reformative step by the administration.

Ponder over the situation and suggest effective ways to tackle each of the above mentioned problems.

Step-1: *Issues—Negligence, dereliction of duty, corruption, indiscipline.*
Step-2: *Dilemma—The administrative situation requires urgent strong action to maintain quality health service delivery, but it might lead to friction with the staff and union and may affect the health services due to strikes.*
Step-3: *Take a head-on collision course with the doctors, staff and enforce discipline.*
1. *Take a practical approach to dealing with the complex administrative situation.*

Step-4: *This is a typical situation in government set-up. In the case of a hospital, it is very difficult to deal with the strike of the employees as the health services will be affected leading to many casualties and immense public pressure. Therefore, a balanced long-term strategy should be adopted.*

The primary stakeholders in this case are the patients and local citizens. Involving the stakeholders will ensure a strong constituency for the reforms to improve the health service delivery. Secondly, the support of the top officials in the district is essential to tackle any untoward situations arising out of strong action against the staff. Therefore, the starting point to initiate the reforms is the Rogi Kalyan Samiti. Every district hospital has a Rogi Kalyan Samiti, normally headed by the District Collector. The strategy should be to take the Collector into confidence, ensure participation of the eminent citizens of the town and the civil society in the Rogi Kalyan Samiti meetings. Then tackle the issues in the hospital management one by one through discussion and passing resolution in the Rogi Kalyan Samiti meetings.

1. Hygiene and housekeeping activities are better managed through outsourcing. Take measure to outsource following all transparent procedures.
2. Put up boards at all the important locations in the campus asking patients not to pay bribe and mobile numbers of Medical Superintendent/District Collector be displayed to inform in case of any harassment. Then based on the reports and complaints, trap some staff red-handedly, with the help of the District Collector and Superintendent of Police. This should be followed up by strict disciplinary action. And ensure vigilance regularly. This will instil fear in the minds of the staff.
3. Medical negligence cannot be tolerated as it leads to loss of valuable life. This should be made clear in all meetings repeatedly. At the first instance of any case of medical negligence leading to a casualty, a criminal liability case along with disciplinary

proceedings should be initiated. The message has to be loud and clear that medical negligence will not be tolerated.

4. Proper accountability system with check and balances should be put in place to account for every medicine in the hospital stock. Computerization along with regular inspection mechanism should be ensured. A vigilance squad can be formed along with the Rogi Kalyan Samiti members to make surprise checking. Action should be initiated on the staff involved.
5. The issue should be discussed in Rogi Kalyan Samiti meetings and resolution passed against such practices and expressing a will to take strong action against the doctors deviating from the service norms. Since the senior doctors attend the Samiti meetings, the message will be clear to them. A vigilance team should be formed to collect evidences against the main doctors who indulge in this practice and show-cause notices should be issued.

   If still the practice continues, the disciplinary proceedings should be initiated against the errant doctors. Simultaneously, with the help of District Collector, the private nursing homes should be sent notices for harassment of the poor patients and indulging in unethical medical practices. A general atmosphere of fear will be created both in the doctors and the nursing homes. This should be followed up regular vigilance and also an inspection mechanism to check the performance of every doctor like say how many patients were attended to operate etc. An MIS will be helpful in tracking the doctors' performance.
6. The Union will no doubt try to create obstacles and resist any reform measure. You should have an emergency plan in case of strike by the staff and doctors. It included requisition of doctors and staff from neighbouring districts. The pressure of Rogi Kalyan Samiti and the District administration will ensure implementation of the above measures. In the worst case scenario, the Essential Services Maintenance Act (ESMA) can be imposed to check breakdown in health services due to a strike.

So, please note that given the time and space constraint in Examination, it is impossible to allot lot of time for a single question, and it is not feasible to write the lengthy answers as above. The points in earlier paragraphs are given only to understand the practical administrative issues. A short and clear answer is always appreciated.

CASE STUDY: 1

Mr. X works as an auto-rickshaw driver in Delhi. Recently, the Delhi government has mandated that no auto-rickshaw shall deny service to any commuter, and that anyone doing so would lose his/her commercial driving license and would also have to pay a heavy fine. One night, Mr. X got a phone call from his wife that their son is critically ill and he must reach home immediately. As Mr. X prepares to rush for home, a young woman asks him to drop her to the airport. The airport is about 30 km in exactly opposite direction to Mr. X's home, and if he chooses to go to the airport, he would not be able to attend to his son in time, and the delay can be fatal for his son. The lady is repeatedly requesting him to help her because it is very late in the night and she is not feeling safe.

She says that if he refuses to drop her to the airport, she will complain to the police and Mr. X's driving license may be suspended.

Questions

1. Identify the ethical and moral dilemma in this case.
2. What are the options available before Mr. X?
3. Which option should he choose and why?
4. In such cases where one has to choose between private and professional life, what should be the objective criteria for taking a decision?

CASE STUDY: 2

You are the District Magistrate of a town, which has seen communal clashes in recent past. Though the clashes are in control right now, the situation is still tense. In the meantime, 'Ramnavami'—a festival of Hindus—is coming up, where the devotees take out loud processions on foot, through the streets of the city. In normal years, the procession takes a route that passes through a Muslim-majority area. But this year, you are conscious that in a communally charged atmosphere, such a route may fuel further tension between the two communities. However, when you sit down with the district administration team to prepare an alternate route for the procession, you realize that the shortest alternate route is at least 15 kilometres longer than the traditional route. Such a long route would not be practical for the devotees and is bound to face strong opposition from the Hindu group.

Questions

1. What would you do? Evaluate the below options:
   a. Insist on the longer route and try to convince the Hindu groups.
   b. Continue with the traditional route, with enhanced security measures.
   c. Cancel the procession ritual for this year's Ramnavami.
2. Any other option(s) you may suggest. Which one would you choose and why? Give reasons.

CASE STUDY: 3

You are the Superintendent of Police of a backward tribal district, which is infamous for child labour. Ever since you joined office, you have taken strict action against hotels and restaurants employing children. One day, the Police Commissioner invites you for a dinner at his residence, and there, you are shocked to see that a 12-year-old tribal girl is employed as a domestic help at your boss's house. You object about this to the Commissioner, but he takes it very lightly and says that he treats her like his own daughter, ensures education at home for her and his wife delegates very 'light' tasks to the girl. You, however, insist that this is against the law—to which the Commissioner threatens you with dire consequences, including suspension from service. When you enquire about this incident from your colleagues, they advise you to keep away from this case as it involves a senior officer, and its pursuit will ultimately hit a dead-end since the Commissioner can easily manipulate the evidences against him.

Questions

1. What are the options available to you? Identify the merits and demerits of each.
2. Choose the best option and justify your answer.
3. Why do you think senior officers, such as the Commissioner of Police in this case, are often able to defy the law with impunity? Suggest measures to overcome such a situation.
4. In the absence of proper rehabilitation schemes for the rescued child labourers, how justified is it to deprive them of their source of livelihood?

CASE STUDY: 4

You are the Chairman of the Municipal Corporation of a city. Of late, the city has seen a steep rise in the number of dog-bite cases, with more than 5 children succumbing to injuries caused due to biting of street dogs in the last week. The Resident Welfare Associations' (RWAs) representatives meet you and urge you to take action urgently. You have tried to control the menace by sterilizing the dogs, but this has not helped to contain the situation. Moreover, the Municipal Corporation is severely short-staffed and inadequately funded—because of which you are unable to take any long-term measures. The district administration and RWAs have suggested you to consider the option of culling the street dogs. But the animal welfare groups are strictly opposed to such a move, as it is against the nature's laws and infringes upon the rights of animals. They have threatened to launch a citywide strike if the street dogs are culled. Local MLA is also a dog-lover and is totally against culling.

Questions

1. Is this case really a trade-off between human rights and animal rights? Examine.
2. How can this situation be handled peacefully and effectively? Give pragmatic solutions.

CASE STUDY: 5

You are the Executive Engineer in a State Electricity Board (SEB). The SEB is suffering heavy financial losses due to theft of electricity and you have decided to act to curb this menace. In the meanwhile, you come to know about rampant electricity theft in the outskirts of the town. You take a team of law-enforcement officials to that area and notice that indeed, ten to fifteen families are blatantly flouting rules by engaging in electricity theft. When you question these people, you are told that they had applied for a metered electricity connection about 8 months ago. They also show a valid receipt of the application. They, however, allege that the junior engineer in the electricity department is asking for a bribe of ten thousand rupees per house to sanction the metered connection. Since these families are poor, they cannot pay such a hefty bribe. As a result, even after 8 months, they have still not got the connection—while the normal timeframe for issuing fresh connection is 15 days. Moreover, these people have school-going children, and without electricity they cannot study at night. Hence, they say that they have no option but to steal electricity till they get a metered connection.

Questions

1. What would you do in this situation? Evaluate each of the below options with merits and demerits, and suggest the best one with justification –
   (a) Ask the law-enforcement officers to book the people engaged in electricity theft.
   (b) Dismiss the Junior Engineer accused of asking for a bribe.
   (c) Waive the electricity charge for the poor families.
2. How can the SEBs reduce the problem of electricity theft? Suggest one innovative solution.

CASE STUDY: 6

You are posted as the District Officer of a temple town, which holds a Kumbh Mela every 12 years. Pilgrims from all over the country come to the fair—making it one of the largest religious gatherings in Asia. Unfortunately, due to the large volume of the crowd, almost every Kumbh Mela in the past has seen some major or minor incident of stampede and subsequent loss of lives. This year, however, you have resolved to ensure that there are no such incidents and have asked the police, NGOs and religious associations for active cooperation in this regard. You have conducted mock drills, demarcated the slots and areas for different sections of the crowd, and the sequence in which they will take ritualistic 'holy bath' on the final day of the fair.

However, on the final day, you get a phone call from the Chief Minister's Office (CMO) that the CM and his family want to perform the holy bath at the fair. You are asked to ensure that the VIP family gets quick and adequate space for the same. You are in a fix because the request has come too late for you to make proper arrangements. Any alteration in the arrangements now may lead to haphazard crowd movement and a sudden rush among the crowd for the rituals—which has all the possibilities for a catastrophic stampede. You attempt to reason with the CMO, but they are not willing to listen.

Questions

1. Do you think VIPs and their families should get preferential treatment at such fairs? Why or why not?
2. As the District Officer, what are the options before you? Identify the merits and demerits of each. Which option will you choose and why? Give justifications.

CASE STUDY: 7

You are posted as a District Magistrate in a town, which often sees communal clashes. Recently, a movie, based on a sensitive religious issue, was released in the country after getting requisite Censor Board certification. However, after the release of the movie, there has been anger among the minorities who claim blasphemous content in the movie and demand a nationwide ban. The Supreme Court, however, has refused to allow such a pan-India ban. In the meanwhile, minority groups approach you, requesting that the movie not be allowed in the sensitive town. After seeing the movie yourself, you are also convinced that it is derogatory to the minority community. Also, being in-charge of the communally sensitive district, you are concerned about the law and order scenario on the day these movies release.

Questions

1. What would you do? Some of the options to deal with the issue are mentioned below. Evaluate these options and suggest the best course of action, giving your reasons for it.
   (a) Do not allow the release of movie in your district as you feel that it hurts the religious sentiments.
   (b) Make sure the movie is released, but provide additional security forces to prevent any untoward incident.
   (c) Ask for guidance from the superiors.
2. Do you think that the Freedom of Expression should be allowed to be held hostage to religious groups? Justify your answer.

CASE STUDY: 8

Mr. X has recently started working as a cyber-security analyst at a government intelligence organization. During the course of his work, he stumbles upon documents, which reveal that the government is spying on leaders of opposition parties with alleged Maoist links. He discusses this matter with his superior officer who tells him that though the spying was illegal, it was essential for national security. He also tells Mr. X that sanction for the spying came from the highest echelons of the government. He further warns him not to divulge facts of the case to anyone else in the organization and especially no one on the outside as it may lead to his dismissal from the organization or even his arrest for treason. However, Mr. X being an honest person finds himself in a deep conflict. He feels that the spying, apart from being illegal, could also be misused by the government for settling political scores with its opponents.

Questions

1. The following are some options that Mr. X has. Evaluate the merits and demerits of each of these:
   (a) Do nothing, as he does not want to risk losing his job or end up in jail for treason.
   (b) Talk to the head of the organization to get his opinion on the matter and then do as he says.

(c) Send an anonymous letter to the press leaking the details of the case.
(d) Go to the press directly with the details of the case.

2. Also indicate (without necessarily restricting to the above options) what you would like to advise, giving proper reasons.

CASE STUDY: 9

You have recently been voted as the President of the Resident Welfare Association (RWA) of your locality, which is near a prominent coaching hub of the town. Hundreds of students from all over the country come to this region to enrol in the coaching institutes and stay as tenants in the nearby areas. During the weekly meetings with the residents of the colony, you notice that there is a strong anti-minority feeling amongst them. They have in fact given you a written memorandum to ensure that no Muslim tenant is allowed in their colony. Even though you have explained to the residents that such an act is inappropriate both on social and legal grounds, they are adamant. In the meanwhile, you hear about many cases in the neighbourhood where Muslim students are being denied rented accommodation.

Questions

In the above context, answer the following:

1. What can be the reasons for even well-educated people often having such a communally-biased attitude? Can their attitude be justified based on a history of communal violence in their families?
2. How can the values of compassion and empathy be inculcated in such people? Give one pragmatic solution.
3. How can you effectively handle the above situation?

CASE STUDY: 10

You have recently joined as the District Magistrate (DM) of a city. This is your first posting as a DM and you are eagerly looking forward to the experience. However, few months into the job, you start feeling frustrated with the overall inefficiency of the staff and their lack of commitment for public service. In your routine surveys to other government offices of the city, you notice a similarly dull work culture—with problems like non-punctuality, absenteeism, lack of cleanliness, improper handling of files and records and so on. You are also aware that this kind of work culture is resulting in inefficient delivery of services to the people. When you take up this matter with your senior officer, he says that as a young officer, you have a great opportunity to improve the condition and develop your city as a 'model city'—which can be emulated by others.

Questions

Answer the following questions:

1. In the above case, what steps would you take to improve the work culture in the government offices of your city?

2. Suppose that while you are implementing your steps with great zeal and sincerity, you are abruptly transferred to a different city. You also come to know that your successor would not be interested in carrying forward your measures and in fact may not be bothered at all about work culture.
   (a) What would you do in this situation?
   (b) Will it lead to loss of motivation in you? How will you maintain your motivation level?

CASE STUDY: 11

You are collector of a district. One day, you come to hear the shocking news that in a village, within the legal jurisdiction, 5 people were killed and 25 arrested for a crime. The situation is tense in that village. There is a possibility of counter retaliation and the murders could continue unabated unless a solution to the problem is found. On visiting the spot of the crime, located in the fields almost at the village boundary, you discover further that the cattle of one party would go along the field bunds of the other parties' land in order to reach the pasture land at the village boundary. The field owners objected to this because they felt that the cattle have caused damage to their crops. The record of customary rights of the villagers permitted people to use bunds to move their cattle around. Therefore, when the field owners stopped the movement of cattle, the cattle owners became annoyed. As a result, the fracas developed and 5 of the field owners were killed. In turn, 25 of the cattle owners were in custody on a murder charge.

Questions

1. How will you solve the case and what steps will you take to ensure that the root cause of the problem is addressed and there is no more violence on this issue?

CASE STUDY: 12

The Minor Irrigation Department of a State Government sanctions huge funds to the District Rural Development Agency (DRDA), of which the District Collector is the Chairman. The District Collector provides irrigation tubewells to small and medium farmers at a time of unprecedented droughts.

The scheme is to give 1/3rd subsidy from the fund, get 2/3rd from the individual farmer and sink the tubewell in the particular farmer's land under District Collector's general supervision. The Collector has to ensure timely action and good quality tube wells.

The Managing Director of DRDA and the Executive Engineer of Minor Irrigation Department in the district are not in good terms and are labelling charges of incompetence and previous malpractices against each other. Each approaches you (as if you are the Collector) to allocate the entire funds exclusively at his disposal for implementing the scheme.

Your number two, the District Development Officer (who is on verge of retirement), who is also the Vice-Chairman of DRDA, is non-committal and leaves it to you to decide how to implement the scheme. Time is running out due to the extreme drought conditions.

Question

1. How will you proceed to implement the scheme?

CASE STUDY: 13

More than a dozen PILs (Public Interest Litigations) are filed in High Court of a State by few people and NGOs alleging large-scale irregularities, malpractices, abuse of authority and misappropriation of huge public funds for private gains by organized groups in Government with close nexus with political executives of the State Government. All PILs are praying for CBI inquiry, as The State Police and Vigilance Department will not conduct fair enquiry against big wigs in the state government, who are themselves involved in the huge scandal.

As senior civil servant of the State Government, you are directed by the State Government to sign statement of facts of the cases as drafted by senior officers (including your service colleagues) of various Departments and file affidavit in the High Court, informing the High Court about the facts of the cases and opposing CBI inquiry, as the State Government is competent and sincere to punish the guilty without any favour or fear.

Question

1. What will you do in such situation?

CASE STUDY: 14

You are head of an organization engaged in research and development of cutting-edge technologies in electronics, essential for economic and security needs of our country. You have a dedicated team which is highly motivated also and has been giving desired outcomes. Your quality control unit's head is Mr. Sharma, a very competent person and honest to his job.

One day, a junior lady scientist working under Mr. Sharma came to you and wanted to lodge the complaint against him. She told you that for last few days Mr. Sharma has been making undue advances towards her, and when she expressed her opposition to such a behaviour, he is threatening her to keep quiet or he will ruin her career. She also told you that if the problem is not shorted out, she will formally lodge a complaint to the police in this regard.

Questions

1. What options you are left with?
2. Which option will you consider as solution and why?

CASE STUDY: 15

Recently you have taken charge as the head of a government organization. On the first day in your office, you observed that the organization is facing irregularities, such as:

i. The staff is not punctual.
ii. The staff waste their time in gossips.
iii. There is no prompt action on public grievances.
iv. The corruption in office is rampart at all levels.
v. The quality of service provided by the organization is low.

Questions

1. What actions would you take to resolve above problems?
2. What will you do to ethically motivate your staff?

CASE STUDY: 16

You are head of an organization. Your junior officer working just below you is arrogant, ill-tempered and poor manager. His levels of achievements are low.

You have to write his ANNUAL CONFIDENTIAL REPORT (ACR) at the end of the financial year. You are aware that he will come to know about your written comments. He will continue to work in your team for indefinite time, over which you have no control. A bad ACR is bound to weaken his future promotion and annoy him against you.

Question

1. What kind of ACR you will write?

CASE STUDY: 17

You are a doctor in the night shift looking after the emergency unit of a hospital. A female patient is rushed into the emergency ward while you are in charge of the ward. You are a conscientious doctor recognized for saving lives in this unit, and your reputation is built on the foundation of several years of service you have provided to those who faced life and death situations under your care. The patient is a victim of a traumatic accident and needs immediate blood transfusion to save her life. However, she belongs to a Christian community whose religion forbids her from taking blood into her body from outside. She is represented by her relatives and priests of her denomination, who do not permit blood transfusion.

Question

1. What will you do and why?

CASE STUDY: 18

Mr. Pandey is working as a jailor of a jail. As part of his duty, he gets the opportunity to interact with the inmates. In course of his interaction with the inmates, he is especially impressed by one of the inmates. It is revealed to him that the prisoner is not a hard-core criminal. A minor incident leading to accidental murder led to his incarceration. He has a family to look after with minor kids. Without Mr. Singh's realization, he ends up developing emotional attachment with the prisoners as between an elder brother and his younger brother. One day, he notices that he has indulged in a violent fight with other prisoners. The jailor thinks, the prisoner is innocent and wants to help. Mr. Singh also wants to help him fight his case further so as to minimize his punishment.

Questions

1. What should Mr. Pandey do and why?
2. Should he help him or not to prove his innocence in the crime for which he is being punished and why?

CASE STUDY: 19

Your friend is an editor of a newspaper. He is free, fair and impartial in his opinions. He is independent minded and writes independently free of fear and favour on any issue. Due to his independent nature, he has landed into controversy several times earlier. He wants to write an editorial piece on Kashmir. In his writing, he wants to take the position that the fate of Kashmir should be left upon the people of Kashmir. His arguments are that referendum is the best democratic way to decide upon the fate of people. The democratic aspiration of the people can no longer be suppressed as was evident in Soviet Russia and many other Eastern European nations. However, he is also aware that this kind of argument can raise controversies and could possibly threaten his life. Yet he is independent minded and does not fear personal harm coming as a consequence of speaking up the truth.

Questions

1. Advise your friend on the possible course of action for him. Should or shouldn't he write the article?
2. Is it unethical to speak up one's mind? Is his opinion on Kashmir morally correct?

CASE STUDY: 20

AIDS (Acquired Immunodeficiency Syndrome) afflicts 38 million people worldwide. Almost 3 million people died from AIDS in 2003 alone, and over 20 million have died since the epidemic began. A vaccine that could prevent or slow down the spread of this deadly disease would be a boon to the world. However, since 1981 when the first cases of AIDS were diagnosed, researchers have been unsuccessful in their attempts to develop such a vaccine. The efforts of a company called VaxGen illustrate the complexity of this task.

VaxGen, which is located in Brisbane, California, developed a vaccine called AIDSVAX. The vaccine contained synthetic proteins of recombinant gp120, a protein normally found on the surface of HIV, the virus that causes AIDS. The vaccine was designed to induce the immune system to respond to this non-infectious protein and to produce antibodies that could protect the recipient from an actual HIV infection. In phase I clinical trials, the vaccine was tested for safety. Phase II clinical trials included a larger-scale test for safety as well as a test for the production of antibodies against gp120. As a result of these trials, AIDSVAX was shown to be safe, and patients receiving the vaccine did develop antibodies against gp120.

Phase III clinical trials involved large-scale, placebo-controlled, double-blind tests of the vaccine's effectiveness. The first trial began in June of 1998 and involved 5,100 gay men and 300 women, all volunteers, from the United States, Puerto Rico, Canada and the Netherlands. The second trial began in March of 1999 and involved 2,500 IV drug abusers from Bangkok, Thailand. Both trials were completed in 2003. Unfortunately, these trials revealed no difference in the overall rate of HIV infection between the vaccinated and the unvaccinated participants. The data indicate that recipients of the vaccine did produce antibodies against gp120, but that those antibodies were not adequate to protect against HIV infection. (It did appear that certain subgroups—ethnic minorities other than Hispanic—exhibited a small but statistically significant lowering of the infection rate, but these results are still being examined.)

Questions

1. Why do you think a person would volunteer to test an AIDS vaccine?
2. In the AIDSVAX trials, some people were given a placebo instead of the vaccine. All the recipients had been told of this possibility ahead of time, but they did not know which substance they were receiving. Is it ethical to give some of the trial participants only a placebo?

CASE STUDY: 21

You have recently joined as the head of a district-level government office, which registers the unemployed people of the district and provides necessary help and guidance so that they can get gainful employment. When you join, you find that the office keeps its resources in a very poorly organized manner. Many rooms of the office are full of dirt, files and records are randomly stacked and many files are virtually thrown across the Record Room, roof of which also leaks in rains. The subordinate officials are very rude to the visitors and ask money for providing various services to the youth who come for seeking information and assistance. As head of the organization, what will be your specific response to the following? Also, provide answers with proper justifications.

Questions

1. What step will you take for keeping the files and records in proper order?
2. What will be your specific action for creating a suitable grievance redressal mechanism?
3. How will you try to improve the work culture of your office?

CASE STUDY: 22

Rajiv is newly posted as secretary in a Panchayat. Within few days he got a circular which said that he should soon conduct Grama Sabha to finalize the action plan of MGNREGA. Action plan contains the list of works to be undertaken in the villages and their estimated expenditures. This should be decided in the Grama Sabha, and the decision of Gram Sabha is immutable.

The Gram Sabha was held and chairman, all elected members, officer in-charge, engineer and people from villages debated and finally listed important works to be undertaken, and the estimated expenditure was decided there itself.

Next, this plan had to be approved in the Panchayat meeting and sent to Tehsil for further approval for sanction of funds. The chairman of Panchayat, who was also a class-I contractor, met Rajiv and asked him to manipulate the funds estimates. Even few members who themselves were small-time contractors and who had previously used machines in MGNREGA scheme to finish works and draw money joined Chairman in demanding manipulation of the action plan.

Rajiv strongly objected to this. On the day of meeting, which was a close-door meeting inside the Panchayat office, he was manhandled by some members in the office after he resisted their attempt to snatch the action plan and manipulate it, and was threatened that if he didn't act according to their orders, he would be thrashed again and again. Someone outside called the police. But when police arrived, the chairman alleged that Panchayat secretary behaved in an indecent manner with female members and hence he was thrashed. Female members seconded this allegation.

Rajiv was taken to police station. Police refused to accept his version of the incident, which was true. He was helpless at the moment.

Question

1. You are his superior officer i.e. BDO. Rajiv contacts you and tells you his part of the story. At the same time, Panchayat members narrate their version. How will you proceed from here?

CASE STUDY: 23

Your close friend, Asit, successfully cleared the prestigious civil service examination and was excited about the opportunity that he would get through the civil services to serve the country. However, soon after joining the services, he realized that things are not as rosy as he had imagined.

He found a number of malpractices prevailing in the department assigned to him. For example, funds under various schemes and grants were being misappropriated. The official facilities were frequently being used for personal needs by the officers and staffs. After some time, he noticed that the process of recruiting staffs was also not up to the mark. Prospective candidates were required to write an examination in which a lot of cheating was going on. Some candidates were provided external help in the examination. Asit brought these incidents to the notice of his seniors. However, he was advised to keep his eyes, ears and mouth shut and ignore all these things which were taking place with the connivance of the seniors. Asit felt highly disillusioned and uncomfortable. He comes to you seeking your advice.

Question

1. Indicate various options that you think are available in this situation. How would you help him to evaluate these options and choose the most appropriate path to be adopted?

CASE STUDY: 24

You are an honest and sincere officer. You have been transferred to a remote district to head a Department that is notorious for its inefficiency and callousness. You find that the main cause of the poor state of affairs is the indiscipline of a section of employees. They do not work themselves and also disrupt the working of others. You first warned the troublemakers to mend their ways or else face disciplinary action. When the warning had little effect, you issued a show cause notice to the ring leaders. As a retaliatory measure, these troublemakers instigated a women employee amongst them to file a complaint of sexual harassment against you with the Women Commission. The Commission promptly sought your explanation. The matter is also publicized in the media to embarrass you further. Some of the options to handle this situation could be as follows:

i. Give your explanation to the Commission and go soft on the disciplinary action.
ii. Ignore the Commission and proceed firmly with the disciplinary action.
iii. Brief your seniors, seek directions from them and act accordingly.

Question

1. Suggest other possible option(s). Evaluate all of them and suggest the best course of action, giving your reasons for the same.

CASE STUDY: 25

Suppose you are the CEO of a company that manufactures specialized electronic equipment used by a Government Department. You have submitted your bid for the supply of this equipment to the Department. Both the quality and cost of your offer are better than those of the competitors. Yet the concerned officer is demanding a hefty bribe for approving the tender. Getting the order is important both for you and your company. Not getting the order would mean closing a production line. It may also affect your own career. However, as a value conscious person, you do not want to give any bribe.

Question

1. Valid arguments can be advanced both for giving the bribe and getting the order, and for refusing to pay bribe and risking the loss of the order. What could be those arguments? Could there be any better way to get out of this dilemma? If so, outline the main elements of this third way, pointing out its merits.

CASE STUDY: 26

You are head of an organization in Central Government. 'A', an IAS Officer, is reporting to you and 'B', an IRTS Officer on deputation to your department, is reporting to 'A' in the same organization. 'B' complains to you repeatedly that 'A' is in the habit of harassing him and is also threatening him that 'A' will ruin his records by writing adverse remarks. 'B' pleads before you to shift him out of 'A's' control and let him work under another officer, or he will go back to his parent cadre prematurely, even before his deputation tenure ends.

You know that 'B' is a good officer. You would like to keep him in your department. But allowing the request of 'B' and transferring 'B' out of the control of 'A' and placing him, i.e. 'B' under another senior officer in your department is sure to annoy 'A', who will continue to work under you.

Question

1. In such a scenario, how will you act to the plea of 'B'?

CASE STUDY: 27

A person has taken charge as an Additional District Magistrate (ADM). He realizes that there is huge corruption in the Public Distribution System (PDS). He also watched that corruption is also widespread in various schemes of development, such as rural roads, bridges and clearing silt from the ponds. Due to widespread corruption, people of the District find themselves hopeless and feel insecure.

This Additional District Magistrate decided to act firmly against aforementioned malpractices. He raided the PDS shops to expose the corrupt dealers and take action by cancelling the quota itself wherever he finds abnormalities. He has also taken stern actions against corrupt contractors who were responsible for not executing properly the development schemes. He has also enforced the rule of law in the district under his proper supervision.

As a result of appropriate actions taken by the A.D.M., the P.D.S. began to work properly and the people got their fair share of ration from P.D.S. outlets. Also, they got better quality of roads and improved law and order conditions in the district. All these actions resulted in an improved quality of governance and re-established public faith in the administration.

Questions

In the context of above case study, answer the questions given below:

1. Which type of Administrative and moral value you see in the above administrator?
2. What was the basic problem of that District?
3. If you were on the same post, what type of actions would you have taken?

CASE STUDY: 28

You have just taken charge as the Director in an important Ministry of Government of India which is responsible for carrying out development schemes worth the value of thousands of crores of rupees. On the very first day of joining as the Director of the Department, you called a meeting of all your subordinate officers and staffs. You found out that two of your subordinate officers of the rank of Deputy Director, Mr. 'A' and Mr. 'B', are absent. You also noticed that Section Officers, Mr. 'C' and Mr. 'D', are not at good terms with one another. The other staffs also seemed to be demotivated.

At the afternoon of the same day, your superior officer of the level of Joint Secretary called you in his office. He discussed with you a very important new project (of thousands of crores rupees) that must be launched as soon as possible in your supervision. He also asked you to insure its effective and speedy implementation.

You have doubts whether the present team will be able to properly handle the project.

Question

1. What would you do in the present situation and why?

CASE STUDY: 29

Suppose one of your close friends, who is aspiring for Civil Services, comes to you for discussing some of the issues related to ethical conduct in public service. He raises the following points:

i. In present time, when unethical environment is quite prevalent, individual attempts to stick to the ethical principles may cause a lot of problems in one's career. It may also cause hardships to the family members as well as risks to one's life. Why should not we be pragmatic and follow the path of least resistance and be happy by doing whatever good we can?
ii. When so many people are adopting wrong means and are grossly harming the system, what difference would it make, if only a very small minority tries to be ethical? The fact remains that they are going to be rather ineffective and are bound to get frustrated in long run.

iii. If we become very fussy about the ethical considerations, will it not hamper the economic progress of our country? After all, in the present age of high competition, we cannot afford to be left behind in the race for further development.

iv. It is understandable that we should not get involved into the grossly unethical practices. But giving and accepting small gratifications and doing small favours increase every body's motivation. It also makes the system more efficient. Then the issue remains that what is wrong in adopting such practices?

Question

1. Critically analyse the above viewpoints. On the basis of such analysis, what will be your advice to your friend?

CASE STUDY: 30

You are placed as 'Qualify Control Officer' in the Ministry of Defence, Government of India. In a recently organized defence expo, you happen to meet your college day friend. He is currently working as 'Marketing Executive' with a well-known company which supplies important defence instruments and components. Your friend invites you for a dinner which you accept. During the dinner, your friend makes a good offer to you. But you humbly deny the offer and tell him that you are not going to quit the job. After a pause, he tells you that it was not his intention that you should quit the job. But he only wants that in near future, when there is going to be huge defence procurement deal, you should help him so that his company successfully gets major chunk of that deal. He also offers you a 10% cut of the deal amount to you as incentive. And he also tells you that being an old friend, he will keep everything secret in future.

Questions

1. What option will you choose from the options given below? And why?
   (i) You are not in hurry to make money. So, you will tell about this lucrative under the table offer to your colleagues.
   (ii) You are an honest person and you feel badly hurt by this offer of your friend. You also know that you have to face this type of situation again and again in this job. So, you try to find another good job and quit this one.
   (iii) You will make a complaint to the police about this incidence involving such a bribe.
2. Suggest any other option you may have.

CASE STUDY: 31

You are appointed as Medical Superintendent at a district-level hospital which provides medical aid and healthcare facilities to the people of the town as well as those of rural areas of the District. The hospital has good infrastructure and is properly equipped with medical instruments required to effectively conduct medical surgical operations. Also, there exists appropriate fund for general and recurring expenditures. However, you find that patients are regularly complaining about the following in that hospital:

i. Housekeeping of the hospital premises is very poor and unhygienic.
ii. The hospital personnel often demand bribe to provide facilities.
iii. On many occasions, the grave carelessness by the Doctors causes death of the patients.
iv. Huge amount of the hospital medicine is sold out by the hospital staff illegally to private medical stores.
v. There is a nexus between doctors and private nursing homes and testing labs, due to which patients are forced to buy costly medicines and undertake costly and often unrequired medical tests.
vi. There exists a defamed workers' union which opposes all the efforts of positive reforms.

Question

After properly assessing the above situations, what measures will you take to improve the overall condition of hospital?

CASE STUDY: 32

You are working as an Executive Engineer in the construction cell of a Municipal Corporation. You are presently in-charge of the construction of a flyover. There are two Junior Engineers under you who have the responsibility of day-to-day inspection of the site and are reporting to you, while you are finally reporting to the Chief Engineer who heads the cell. While the construction is heading towards completion, the Junior Engineers have been regularly reporting that all constructions are taking place exactly as per the design specifications. However, in one of your surprise inspections, you noticed some serious deviations and lacunae, which in your opinion are likely to affect the safety of the flyover. Rectification of these lacunae at this stage would require a substantial amount of demolition and rework which will cause a tangible loss to the contractor and will also delay completion. There is a lot of public pressure on the Corporation to get this construction completed because of heavy traffic congestion in the area. When you brought this matter to the notice of the Chief Engineer, he advised you that in his opinion it is not a very serious lapse and may be ignored. He advised for further expediting the project for completion in time. However, you are convinced that this was a serious matter which might affect public safety and should not be left unaddressed.

Question

What will you do in such a situation? Some of the options are given below. Evaluate the merits and demerits of each of these options and finally suggest what course of action you would like to take? Give reasons.

i. Follow the advice of the Chief Engineer and go ahead.
ii. Make an exhaustive report of the situation, bringing out all facts and analysis along with your own viewpoints stated clearly, and then seek written orders from the Chief Engineer in this regard.
iii. Seek explanations from the Junior Engineers and issue orders to the contractor for necessary correction within targeted time.
iv. Highlight the issue to an extent so that it reaches superiors to the Chief Engineer.
v. Considering the rigid attitude of the Chief Engineer, seek transfer from the projector report sick and stay away on medical leave.

CASE STUDY: 33

You are heading a leading technical institute of the country. The institute is planning to convene an interview panel shortly under your chairmanship for selection of the post of professors. A few days before the interview, you get a call from the Personal Secretary (PS) functionary seeking your intervention in favour of the selection of a close relative of the functionary for this post. The PS also informs you that he is aware of the long-pending and urgent proposals of your institute for grant of funds for modernization, which are awaiting the functionary's approval. He assures you that he would get these proposals cleared.

Questions

1. What are the options available to you?
2. Evaluate these options and choose the option which you would adopt, giving reasons.

CASE STUDY: 34

As a senior officer in the Finance Ministry, you have access to some confidential and crucial information about policy decisions that the government is about to announce. These decisions are likely to have far-reaching impact on the housing and construction industry. If the builders have access to this information beforehand, they can make huge profits. One of the builders has done a lot of quality work for the government and is known to be close to your immediate superior, who asks you to disclose this information to the said builder.

Questions

1. What are the options available to you?
2. Evaluate each of these options and choose the option which you would adopt, giving reasons.

CASE STUDY: 35

You are posted as a senior Labour Enforcement Officer in Sivakashi in Tamil Nadu. Sivakashi is known for its manufacturing clusters on firecrackers and matches. The local economy of the area is largely dependent on firecrackers industry. It has led to tangible economic development and improved standard of living in the area.

So far as child labour norms for hazardous industries like firecrackers industry are concerned, International Labour Organization (ILO) has set the minimum age as 18 years. In India, however, this age is 14 years.

The units in industrial clusters of fire crackers can be classified into registered/non-registered units, and it does not include household-based works. Household-based works mean children working under supervision of their parents/relatives. To evade child labour norms, several units project themselves as household-based works but employ children from outside. Needless to say that employing children saves the costs for these units leading to higher profits to the owners.

On your visit to one of the units which have about 10-15 children below 14 years of age, the owner tells you that in this household-based unit, all the children are his relatives. You notice that several children smirk, when the owner tells you this. On deeper inquiry, you figure out that neither the owner not the children are able to satisfactorily establish their relationship with each other.

Questions

1. What would be your reaction after the visit?
2. Bring out and discuss the ethical issues involved in the above case.

CASE STUDY: 36

A Public Information Officer (PIO) has received an application under the RTI Act. Having gathered the information, the PIO discovers that the information pertains to some of the decisions taken by him, which were found to be not altogether right. There were other employees also, who were party to these decisions. Discloser of the information is likely to lead to disciplinary action, with possibility of punishment against him as well as some of his colleagues. Non-disclosure or part disclosure or camouflaged discloser of information will result either into lesser punishment or in no punishment.

The PIO is otherwise an honest and conscientious person, but this particular decision, on which the RTI application has been filed, turned out to be wrong. He comes to you for advice.

The following are some suggested options:

i. PIO could refer the matter to his superior officer and seek his advice and act strictly in accordance with the advice, even though he is not completely in agreement with the advice of the superior.

ii. The PIO could proceed on leave and leave the matter to be dealt by his successor in office or request for transfer of the application to another PIO.

iii. The PIO could weigh the consequences of disclosing the information truthfully, including the effect on his career, and reply in a manner that would not place him or his career in jeopardy, but at the same time a title compromise can be made on the contents of the information.

iv. The PIO could consult his other colleagues who are party to the decision and take action as per their advice.

Questions

1. Evaluate the merits and demerits of each of the above options.
2. Also please indicate (without necessarily restricting to the above option) what you would like to advise, giving proper reasons.

CASE STUDY: 37

You have taken charge of Block-level officer. You are made in-charge of developmental works in the Block. During your travel through the area, you found that people are living in inhuman conditions, deprived of basic sanitation and drinking water facilities. The commercial banks have not any sympathy towards the farmers, so that the business of money lenders is flourishing. Local MLA also ignores the people who had not voted in favour of him.

Question

1. What should you do as a Block-Level Officer, so that the following points can be addressed?
   a. It can be assured that poor and needy people get help from the Banks.
   b. Drinking water and sanitation service provided by the Panchayati Raj Institution can be made effective especially for the weaker section people.
   c. Ill effect of development project selected in bipartisan manner by local M.L.A. can be mitigated.
   d. The people become aware about their rights and various government schemes of welfare and development.

CASE STUDY: 38

Mid-Day Meal (MDM) is a government programme which deals with supplementary nutrition support through educational Institutions. It took its root in India when Madras Corporation developed a school lunch programme in 1925. In Post-Independent India, the State of Gujarat also started the school lunch programme in 1984. In 1995, a Programme of Nutritional Support of Primary Education was launched at the national level. In 2004, this programme was revised and was popularly known as MDM. Government of India emphasized MDM's implementation in its Common Minimum Programme. It envisaged the provisions of cooked nutritional mid-day meal to primary and secondary school children. This initiative became the world's biggest school lunch program with following objectives:

(a) To improve health and education
(b) To increase school enrolment

(c) To improve socialization
(d) To solve malnutrition problem among young children
(e) Social empowerment of women by employment generation

However, problems of MDM currently include:

(a) poor infrastructure facilities
(b) repetition of same menu
(c) disruption of classroom as teachers are required to oversee the operation
(d) poor quality of food
(e) poor hygiene
(f) inadequate payments to contractors
(g) insufficient budgetary allocation
(h) caste and religious bias
(i) limited parental participation
(j) irregular and delayed delivery
(k) low quality supplies by Food Corporation of India (FCI)
(l) lack of maintenance

The fact remains that, in India, the welfare economies do not work properly. It works for people who create it and for the subordinates who are in position to implement such policies in the public. Political party in power creates such bogus schemes which also benefit the bureaucrats and politicians in power. The current Government, which was in opposition at the time of the implementation of this scheme, never revoked these bogus schemes of the previous government as it did not want to hurt the vote bank.

Questions

1. Should such similar Govt. schemes launched in India in future?
2. How corrupt practices could be prevented most effectively in the case of MDM scheme?

CASE STUDY: 39

Mid-Day Meal (MDM) is a government programme which deals with supplementary nutrition support through educational Institutions. Government of India emphasized MDM's implementation in its Common Minimum Programme. It envisaged the provisions of cooked nutritional mid-day meal to primary and secondary school children. It is also designed to boost school attendance and children's participation in school. This initiative became the world's biggest school lunch programme.

Recently, a State Government constituted a special team to effectively implement the MDM scheme. The mandate of the team is to look into infrastructure issues that include storage facilities, kitchens and quality drinking water. The team comprised of nutritionist, food inspector, dietician, doctor and members from drug-testing laboratories. Mr. Harish is the doctor and his close friend Mr. Mahesh is the food inspector in the said team. The team is supposed to send feedback to the Government after an inspection drive. Both Mahesh and Harish have a lackadaisical approach towards their work. Neither of them is sensing his responsibility properly. They enjoy political patronage in the State. In contrast to them, other team members are quite conscious of their duties and responsibilities. However, they don't have any political connection. Occasionally, the team decision was getting affected by the opinions of the doctor and the food inspector as the duo has close nexus with concerned political boss in the State. Despite some of the lacunae in the infrastructure issues in MDM, positive feedback was sent to the Govt.

Due to the above irresponsible act, quality of food was not ensured and sometimes even contaminated food was served to the children, which resulted in hospitalization of many school children in the State recently.

Questions

1. According to you, who is responsible for the problem highlighted in the above case—both Mahesh and Harish, or team as a whole? Also give reasons.
2. What are the ethical concerns involved in the case?

CASE STUDY: 40

You are the administrative head of a Government Office which deals with the public on a large scale. People regularly come to the office for their routine problems like pension claims, insurance claims, scholarship claims, etc. There is an assistant in the office who deals with these subjects. There is a complaint that he does not clear the claims without extracting a bribe for the same. So far, he has escaped disciplinary action because he has the backing and patronage of a local influential politician. Other assistants of the office are looking towards you for a decisive action. The work culture of the organization has reached to an all-time low efficiency. You have decided to act in the given situation.

Questions

1. What are the various options available to you?
2. Examine the merits and demerits of each option and suggest the best course of action under the given situation.

CASE STUDY: 41

You have recently retired as the financial head of a Public Sector company (PSU) and have joined a private firm as its financial advisor. The PSU has floated tenders for a long-term contract which your firm is interested in. As the financial head of the PSU, you regularly deal with the tender and contract process, and are well aware of the various criteria and parameters on which the PSU awards such contracts. The CEO of your present firm has requested you to use that knowledge in ensuring that the firm bags this contract with PSU, which will significantly boost the firm's revenues. On the other hand, failure to bag the contract may mean shutting down of the firm. The entire team is also looking up to you to disclose the parameters on which the PSU will award contracts to the bidders and is asking you to lead the bidding process.

Questions

1. What are the ethical dilemmas involved in this case?
2. What are the various options available to you? Also examine the merits and demerits of each option and suggest the best course of action under the given situation.

CASE STUDY: 42

You are the Executive Engineer of a road construction department and in charge of construction and maintenance of Major District Roads (MDRs) in a particular district. You have joined this Department recently. In course of your field inspections, you found large-scale misuse of funds in both construction, and in repair and maintenance of MDRs. You have started putting accountability on the concerned Assistant Engineers (AEs) and Junior Engineers (JEs). As a mark of protest, all AEs and JEs have started a 'go-slow' campaign by delaying the work. The financial year is going to close soon and still about 50% of the funds remain un-utilized. Your senior officers have suggested you to explore other options to ensure faster utilization of the funds.

Questions

1. What are the various options available to you?
2. Examine the merits and demerits of each option and suggest the best course of action with reasons.

CASE STUDY: 43

You are an RTI activist. There is a poor person living in a rural area and he wants to get his son admitted to a public school in a city. The public school asks for Transfer and Character Certificates and sets out a deadline for submission, otherwise the boy will not get admission. The father makes desperate attempts to procure the concerned documents, but could not get within the stipulated timeframe and the son is denied of admission. In running from pillar to post, the father met with an accident and lost his two legs. His son meets you and requests to help in redressal of his grievances, including fixing accountability regarding injury to his father. You want to use provisions under RTI Act, 2005.

Questions

1. How would you respond to his request?
2. Suggest some options through which you can help the grieved child.

CASE STUDY: 44

You are the District Magistrate of a backward district, which is ignominious for rampant child labour. One day in your office, an old friend from same school visits you and tells you that he has opened a small restaurant in the town and wants you to come for its inauguration. When you reach there, you notice 2-3 under-fourteen children washing utensils and taking orders. When you enquire from the children, they say that they are very grateful to the hotel owner for employing them, as they are very poor and their parents are too old to support and feed them. The children also tell you that the hotel owner treats them very well and gives them timely food and wages. When you enquire from your friend about employing underage children, he admits to it, but says that if he does not employ them then these children will have no option but to beg on streets.

Questions

1. What are the ethical and legal dilemmas involved in this case?
2. What would be the course of action in the above case? Give reasons.

CASE STUDY: 45

Ramesh is a misogynist from his childhood. However, he is a very diligent and scholar student. He was aspiring to become an IAS Officer from his childhood. By dint of his hard labour, he could fulfil his dream of becoming an IAS Officer. He got posted as a Sub-Divisional Magistrate (SDM) in a District. He was highly committed to and competent in his work. Incidentally, he has to work with a female colleague named Reema, who has been working in the same SDM office for long time now as Private Secretary. Reema has a track record of being one of the most productive employees in that office. But even after being an IAS Officer, Ramesh could not wipe out his misogynistic attitude towards women. He still holds a misperception that women tend to putrefy work culture and have a tendency of social loafing. Because of his inherent stereotyping, he always attributes all misdoings towards Reema. Many a times, Reema has been criticized even for small mistakes.

Questions

1. What are the steps by which Ramesh could be treated for his discriminating attitude?
2. After having known his inherent problem since childhood, what Reema should do to bring him on the right path?
3. Should persons with such perceptions be allowed to hold such high public posts?

CASE STUDY: 46

In a recent tragedy, a cinema hall in your city caught fire leading to death and severe injuries to more than 50 persons. The state orders an immediate inquiry into the incident. You are in charge of the inquiry in your capacity as the district commissioner. In your inquiry, you discover severe lapses made by the cinema hall owners. They had violated norms with respect to safety. They had also violated regulations governing the construction of cinema halls with enough exit doors and emergency exits. The norms on safety from accidental fires were also not met. In other words, if you indict the cinema owners for lapses, they would be charged with homicide, not amounting to murder. However, several state agencies and the officers serving them could also become victims of the report because they let these lapses to continue and were a party to the crime because they allowed the cinema owners or gave them license to operate even when the conditions were not met. You find that you are responsible for the incident because you either did not inspect the cinema hall periodically as required or you couldn't identify the lapses in your inspections.

Question

1. What will you do in such a situation? Some of the options are given below. Evaluate the merits and demerits of each of these options and finally suggest what course of action you would like to take, giving reasons.
   i. You will make a detailed report indicting everyone, including yourself.
   ii. You will seek a legal advice that exonerates you legally and then make a report exonerating yourself.
   iii. You will request to be relieved of your inspection duties, citing your personal responsibility in the accident as a reason.
   iv. You will make a report that holds the cinema owners solely responsible for the case.
   v. You will make a report highlighting the fact that this is one of accident of rarest of rare kind that could not have been avoided thereby minimizing the responsibility on everyone.

CASE STUDY: 47

You are newly posted as a collector in the Malkangiri district of Odisha which is a Naxalite belt. You have empathy to poor and disadvantaged. The district is tribal inhabited and underdeveloped. After having taken charge as the Collector of the District, you noticed that the root cause of Naxalism is the deprivation and backwardness of that district. The government is slightly indifferent to the district. In a recent violence, some Maoists have damaged the public property also. However, one Maoist was caught and confessed that the extreme poverty compelled him to opt for the path of violence.

Questions

1. Would you accept his statement? Why?
2. What course of action you will take against him?

CASE STUDY: 48

You are the Principal of a Government College. One of your close aide named Rajan is a faculty of mathematics. The faculty is highly respected and known for his positive traits.

But one day, a girl student complained of sexual harassment against him. She alleged that the faculty also threatened her that it would harm her studies, if she complained against him. But the girl is neither good in studies nor an obedient student. Several complaints have been registered, many a times, against her. It has been seen in some cases that she was making many false allegations against some students as well as teachers.

Questions

1. Being the Principal of the college, what would be your initial reaction to the girl's statement?
2. How will you proceed with this situation?

CASE STUDY: 49

Suppose you are a Superintendent of Police in a District. You are a highly religious and an ardent supporter of Hindu belief system. In your District, a person, a self-styled godman, started preaching the people regularly in a particular place and persuaded the local people to adopt his principles and follow him as their Guru. With the passage of time, he became very popular and many more became his devotees. In the process, you also became one of his ardent devotees. The self-styled godman has built an ashram too in his name. Suddenly, you hear that the self-styled godman is a fraud and has accumulated much wealth by cheating his devotees. By now, the news has spread among the masses and the mob has turned violent.

Question

1. What steps will be taken by you? Also evaluate the merits and demerits of each step taken by you.

CASE STUDY: 50

The Odisha State Chief Minister seems to be determined to root out corruption in the State and plans to shame those involved in graft cases rather publicly. The CM has decided to post a list of the 'corrupt persons' on the State Vigilance Department's website.

You are the State Vigilance Department chief. You have to cooperate with the CM in this endeavour actively. Among the many featured in the list, there is the name of a Journalist called Chandrabhanu Patnaik, the editor of a local television channel against whom a vigilance case was already filed. Chandrabhanu Patnaik is a friend of your brother, and to your cognizance, he is an honest man. After hearing that his name is in the list to be posted, Chandrabhanu Patnaik comes to you and pleads before you not to make his name public on the website, as he was honest. He also assured you that he was not involved in any corrupt practices and the case in which he was sued was a conspiracy against him.

Question

1. What would be your step in this situation? Give reasons for the step taken by you.

CASE STUDY: 51

You are working with an NGO. You had travelled to one of the villages where your programme is running. In the programme, your funds were fully spent, although your calculations showed that this should not be so. You found that a locally employed Christian accountant had manipulated the accounts. He had grown rich and had many friends. He paid hefty tithes and offerings in the local church. After being confronted about the misappropriation of said funds of NGO, he repaid some money he had taken, but sadly, after more losses were discovered, he committed suicide. His fellow members thought his misdeeds have been reported by their senior most local colleague and were intensely angry with that colleague. Group loyalty was felt more strongly than their obligation to protect institutional funds and, more importantly, the Christian integrity. You boasted that you had detected the fraud and helped rebuild relationships. When you said at his funeral that, 'I had liked and admired our accountant and appreciated his efforts to make good with the losses, and that at the end all of us will need forgiveness'. But you learnt the moral strength of personal loyalty within a group possibly exacerbated because group members thought of themselves as 'poor' nationals dealing with expatriates from a rich country'.

Questions

1. Suggest what could have been done to avoid the scandal in the office?
2. What could have been done by the Church to mitigate the impact of the scandal?

CASE STUDY: 52

You are the Director of Durgapur Ispat Main Hospital. In an incident, four patients, who were admitted to Durgapur Ispat Main Hospital in Burdwan with various problems, became critical after receiving a blood transfusion. In all four cases, the blood was supplied by the hospital's blood bank and the patients' condition deteriorated after the transfusion.

They were shifted to a private facility where they died. The post-mortem report of one patient concluded that she had gone into septic shock following the transfusion. So far, none of the three patients' families have lodged any written complaint with the health department. But, as the news of the deaths of the three spread, the families of other patients started alleging that the hospital's blood bank was supplying contaminated blood. They also accused the hospital of gross negligence, prompting it to set up the probe committee.

Questions

1. Do you think the in-charge of blood bank is responsible for this incident?
2. How will you proceed with the case?

CASE STUDY: 53

You are posted as the District Magistrate (DM) of a Naxal-affected town. One day, while you were on your way to a village to oversee some development work, a group of armed Naxals surrounded the village and abducted you. They blindfolded you and took you to their hideout in the forest. Fortunately, the blindfold was not very tight, and you were able to secretly see through it, without the Naxals knowing. Noticing the path the abductors took, you have managed to identify the exact location of their hideout.

The Naxals kept you kidnapped for one week, after which the State government was able to secure your release safely. However, during your stay with the Naxals, they treated you very nicely. They also discussed with you their problems, and how the government is not doing enough for development of tribal villages. You come to realize that their issues are very genuine. Now, once you have been released, the government is asking for your help in locating the Naxals, so that armed action can be taken against them. You are well aware that if you disclose the location of the Naxals, they would definitely be killed by the Central Police Forces.

Questions

1. Would you disclose the location of the Naxals? Why or why not?
2. What are the other options available before you? Evaluate each of the options with their merits and demerits.

CASE STUDY: 54

You are posted as the Commissioner of Income Tax of an industrial town. A large proportion of the town's population is engaged in business activity, still the tax revenue generated from the town is very minimal—which clearly indicates evasion of taxes by the businessmen. You have decided to take action in this regard and have put an advertisement in the local newspapers that such businessmen should voluntarily pay their tax dues in a 10-day window, after which you will take action against the defaulters. The very next day, representatives of the business association meet you in the office and invite you for inaugurating a new shopping mall in the town. They also give you an idol of Lord Krishna—made in pure gold—as a gift. You suspect that this is a signal for you to go soft on the tax-disclosure front.

Question

1. Below are some of the options available to you. Identify the merits and demerits of each. Which option would you choose and why?
   (a) File a police complaint against the businessmen for attempting to bribe you.
   (b) Take their gift, because it is of a divine God. But you decide not to go to the mall opening.
   (c) Do not accept the gift, but decide to go to the mall opening ceremony.
   (d) Accept their gift and send your junior to the mall opening ceremony.

CASE STUDY: 55

You have recently qualified the Civil Services Exam. with a rank good enough to get into the IPS. Now you are about 32 years old, your parents are eager to get you married. They arrange a match, which is agreeable to you too. However, they are keen on taking on a large sum of money as dowry, and the girl's family has also agreed to the same. When you object to your parent and tell them that taking dowry is illegal, they say your thinking is impractical. They also highlight that you have two unmarried younger sisters, and arranging marriage for them would involve dowry payment. As a brother, you should be responsible to your sisters and even if you don't use your dowry money on yourself, at least it can be used later for the marriage of your sisters. You discuss this issue with your prospective wife, and she tells you not to worry about dowry as her parents have enough money and can easily pay the amount.

Questions

1. What would you do? Evaluate the below options –
   (a) Take the dowry, as it will help in your sisters' marriage.
   (b) Refuse to take the dowry, and lodge a police complaint against your parents and the girl's parents.
   (c) Cancel the marriage and look for another match.
2. How do you think can the young generation of today convince their parents for not taking dowry for their sons' marriage? Give pragmatic solutions.

CASE STUDY: 56

You are an upright and honest police officer, posted in a State infamous for political interference in bureaucracy. As you start taking strict action against crimes in the city, local MPs, MLAs and other local politicians start to victimize you by often talking against you in the media. They are putting lot of pressure on you to let off the arrested criminals. The final straw was when the MLA indirectly hinted that your family might not be safe if you choose not to tow their line. You decide not to remain silent any longer and talk to the media about this victimization. But you are also aware that as per the Civil Service Conduct Rules, going to media in such cases is prohibited.

Questions

1. What are the options available to you?
2. Identify the merits and demerits of each of them, and choose the best one, with justifications.

CASE STUDY: 57

You are posted as the District Magistrate of a town bordering Nepal. After the new Constitution has been adopted in Nepal, the border districts of Nepal are seeing lot of unrest by some groups. Some of this unrest has also spilled over to your town, and the local Nepali-community people are engaging in anti-India protests and sloganeering against alleged lack of action by the Indian government in resolving the crisis in Nepal. Last week, they burnt the Indian flag and even resorted to stone-pelting on the police. The police was forced to open fire in which two Nepali protestors lost their lives. The Central government has asked the state to take immediate measures to bring the situation in control, as it is negatively impacting Indo-Nepal diplomatic ties.

Questions

1. What steps would you take to tackle the situation?
2. Can resorting to firing by the state police be justified in the above case? Give reasons.
3. What long-term measures can you take so that such situations do not recur?

CASE STUDY: 58

You have been recently posted as the District Magistrate of a coastal town in Odisha. There is a warning from the Meteorological Department that a very strong cyclone is coming towards the town and will make a landfall in three days. As you plan to convene an emergency meeting of the District Disaster Management Authority (DDMA), you notice that many of its positions are vacant. Also, the DDMA had not carried out any preparatory or mitigation plans in the town, due to which there is a complete lack of awareness among the people about the 'dos and don'ts' during a cyclone. In the meanwhile, the state government has directed you to ensure that there is no loss of life due to the cyclone.

Questions

1. In this situation, what immediate steps would you take to minimize the damage due to impending cyclone?
2. What are the long-term measures that need to be taken?

CASE STUDY: 59

You have been recently posted as the Station Manager of a major railway station, which handles hundreds of trains per day, and has a daily footfall of over one lakh passengers. However, to your surprise, you notice that the station is drowned in filth, with overflowing dustbins and severe lack of cleanliness in the toilets. When you enquire about this from your staff, they say that they are underpaid and overworked, and they can't possibly handle such a large station. They also complain that the passengers have very poor civic sense and are used to throwing garbage and filth on the station. Meanwhile, under the Swachh Bharat campaign, the Indian Railways has decided to improve cleanliness standards in the platforms, and station managers will be held accountable for any poor implementation of the scheme.

Questions

1 How will you make use of the funds under Swachh Bharat to improve cleanliness at your station? Identify two priority areas for action.
2 Many passengers have a habit of littering on railway platforms. How can it be minimized? Give one innovative solution.

CASE STUDY: 60

You are posted in Uttarakhand as a District Magistrate (DM). The state had recently witnessed a devastating environmental disaster due to reckless construction of buildings and hotels in ecologically fragile regions. As a follow-up measure, the state government has asked all the DMs to re-verify the construction permits of all residential and commercial buildings in such regions. During such re-verification in your district, you come across numerous violations of the norms and decide to take strong action against these builders – including demolition of these illegal structures. However, you notice that many of these illegal buildings are running charitable hospitals and educational institutions also, and demolishing them would take a heavy toll on the health and educational security of the district. Moreover, there is not much alternative land available in the district where these hospitals and schools could be relocated.

Questions

1. What would you do in this situation? Explain the ethical and moral dilemma involved.
2. Is this case a trade-off between social development and environment-protection? Examine.

CASE STUDY: 61

You are posted as the Development Commissioner of a backward state which is running a high budget deficit. After several attempts, the state has managed to convince an international multilateral financial institution to give it a long-term loan at low interest rates. However, financial institution says that the loan is on the condition that the state government would reduce public spending in critical sectors such as education and health, and promote private players in these areas. Additional condition is that private companies should be able to lease land in the state at below-market rates. The state government is strongly opposed to these conditions, but sees no other alternative. As a last-ditch effort, a negotiating team is constituted to convince the financial institution that its demands are unrealistic. You have been appointed the head of this negotiating team.

Questions

1. How would you go about preparing your team for the negotiation? What are the areas you would focus upon during the negotiation?

2. Suppose that despite your best efforts, the lending institution is adamant on the conditions. Now, what would you recommend to the state government – to accept the conditions and take the loan, or to reject the conditions and stay in revenue shortage? Explain.

CASE STUDY: 62

You are the District Magistrate of a town. During your routine inspection to different government offices of the district, you notice that the quality of public service delivery is very poor. Many departments have not put up Citizen's Charters in their offices, and even in those offices where such a charter is present, it is incomplete, not updated and never followed. Public discontent is very high, and for valid reasons. All this is despite the fact that the State government had mandated all public offices to have Citizen's Charters two years ago. You have decided to take this issue on priority.

Questions

1. What are the contents of a good Citizen's Charter?
2. How will you go about the process of ensuring that all public departments have a good Citizen's Charter? Outline the key steps.

CASE STUDY: 63

You are Director and head of an autonomous organization working under a Ministry of Government of India. One of your Joint Directors is very competent and honest to his job. You also liked his way of working. One day he came to you for an important discussion regarding his junior officer recently posted as Deputy Director in his division. During the discussion, the Joint Director has mentioned that the Deputy Director is arrogant and ill tempered. He belonged to SC category and involved in groupism. He is very poor in disposal of his duties and never complete assignments given to him on time. Further, the Joint Director pointed out that the work in the division suffering a lot and immediate action in this matter is required for smooth functioning of the organization.

You sought an explanation about the charges levelled against him from the Deputy Director. The Deputy Director has denied all the charges put against him. On the contrary, he has been alleged of discrimination on the basis of caste. Further, he suspected that the Joint Director will spoil his ACR which will hamper his promotion and seniority. He has demanded action against the Joint Director. He has also threatened that if action is not taken in a week, he will go to SC Commission for seeking justice.

Questions

1. What steps will you take to solve the problem?
2. What will you do to convince both the officers and how?
3. As the matter is sensitive enough, what kind of strategy will you adopt to make conducive environment in the organization?

CASE STUDY: 64

You are head of a project. You appoint several people to complete the related tasks. One of the workers in the team is, however, a troublemaker. He tries to instigate other team members not to devote so much time to finish the assigned tasks in time. He tries to convince his colleagues saying that if they do not delay the project work, the boss will not increase the project duration, and in that case, they will lose their jobs. The trouble is also that, as their boss, you know his clout too to create further troubles in the said project.

Questions

1. What are the options available with you?
2. Which one option you will opt for to rectify the situation? Give reasons.

CASE STUDY: 65

You are an Administrative Officer in an organization. One day, a female worker came to you and she complained that the Assistant Administrative Officer is harassing her. And, the fact remains that the Officer in question is also close to the Head of your organization. The female worker is not a permanent worker, and she is quite vulnerable. She is not covered by the existing labour laws and job security provisions.

She knows that she may be fired if she lodges a written complaint. Your problem is that you cannot do anything without any written complaint from her.

Question

1. In this situation, how you will proceed with her complaint?

CASE STUDY: 66

You are an incharge of a police station. One day, you come to know that one of your junior officer has arrested a boy for committing a murder. The officer has produced the boy before Magistrate in the adult court/session court. As the age of the boy was recorded as more than 18 years in the police report, he was produced in that court. As a result, he was sent to jail. After one year of this incident, one day you come to know the fact that the boy was 17 years old when he committed the said crime and he was wrongly sent to jail. Being a sensitive and committed police officer towards child rights, you enquired into it. You found that the initial mistake was made by your junior officer in your police station. You also come to know that your junior officer was totally ignorant about rules, procedures, roles and responsibilities pertaining to the Juvenile Justice Act. Further, you observed that wrong reporting in the court was mainly responsible for this adverse situation in this case. As a matter of fact, this wrong reporting became the basis of the punishment involved in this case. As per Juvenile Justice Act, if a person found to be below 18 years of age on the date of offence, his case will be transferred to the Juvenile Justice Board and his custody to the Observation Home and he will not be sent to adult court in any case. But unfortunately the action of police was against the law in this case.

Questions

1. How will you ensure that the boy gets justice?
2. What action will you take against your officer?

CASE STUDY: 67

Ratan, a 15-year-old son of an auto driver, was taken to a different village by his friend in pursuit of work. He was employed as a domestic help and he planned to earn some money and return home. He was told that his salary was sent to his father at home, which was not true. After 2 years of enduring hard labour and abuse, Ratan ran away to his village. To his astonishment, he found that his father had expired a year back which was informed to his employer. Being frustrated and confused, Ratan tried to commit suicide, but one of his friends stopped him and took him to an NGO working for the welfare of child labour. Ratan told the incident in detail and requested for action against his employer. The representative of NGO has brought the case before District Labour Welfare Department where you are working as a labour welfare officer.

Questions

1. What will you do in such situation?
2. What are the issues involved in Ratan's case?

CASE STUDY: 68

You recently joined as head of the department in Government of India and responsible for implementation of Support to Training & Employment Programme for women (STEP) of your department. Under this project, your department has already given a grant of 3 crore rupees to an NGO for implementation of this scheme for a period of three years. Just after completion of the project, your department has given an order for evaluation of the project. By this time, the implementing agency has requested to extend the project period for six months. Thereafter, an independent agency has evaluated the project and given its report. The following issues emerged from the findings and recommendations of the report:

i. The project has achieved its objectives to some extent. In terms of number of beneficiaries, selection of target groups has been achieved as per the guidelines.
ii. As envisaged in the scheme, neither monitoring committee of senior officials from state government was formed nor was the implementation of the project monitored.
iii. Support services to the beneficiaries were not provided. The existing available infrastructure could not be utilized due to lack of efforts on the part of the implementing agency.

iv. Federation of SHGs was found formed only on papers while it was necessary to make the federation functional and the involvement of the implementing agency could be minimized and restricted to consultancy only after completion of the project. Thus, sustainability of the project was neglected.

v. As many children of beneficiary families were found engaged in handloom work under the project, they deprived from their education, there is an urgent need to address the child labour problem as well as the educational need of these children.

vi. Cost of administrative expenses of the project was found on higher side. It should be reduced to make the project economic and purposeful.

Questions

1. In view of the above, what steps will you take?
2. What provisions need to be made in the scheme to ensure education for children of beneficiaries?

CASE STUDY: 69

Mohan is the president of the Resident Welfare Association RWA of a society. He has recently received a complaint from a family residing in one of the houses in your society. A religious group has recently rented the ground floor of a house. As a result of their practices, a lot of noise is coming from the house, which is causing disturbance to the family's daily peace. Mohan communicated the problem to the group, and he was assured that they would keep it in control. However, the situation is still the same.

Question

1. What should be the Mohan's next step? Evaluate the below options with merits and demerits:
   (a) Talk to group once again and issue a final warning.
   (b) You would not do anything as every community has the right to follow its religious practices.
   (c) Go to the police and lodge a complaint against the religious group.
   (d) Ask the group to vacate the premises as soon as possible.

CASE STUDY: 70

You are a junior manager at one of the major automobile companies in India. The company has recently introduced some policies, which have adversely affected the wages of the labour force. When you take up this matter with the senior management, they convey to you that such changes were necessary because of the recent losses suffered by the firm. The workers are very aggrieved due to this decision and the trade union has decided to call a strike. Repeated attempts by the senior management to ask the workers to join work have failed, and they now have chosen you as a mediator to negotiate with the workers.

Questions

1. What are the various options available to you by which you can balance the interests of workers and the firm?
2. Evaluate each of these options and choose the best one, with justifications.

CASE STUDY: 71

You are working as a software engineer in a leading software development firm. You were part of a global team working on a very critical module, with very stringent timelines. One day before the project deadline, during routine testing of the module, you notice that there are some issues in the code written by your team, which could adversely affect the functionality of the module. Fixing this issue will take at least a week. You report this issue to the project manager, but he insists that since the affected functionality will be used very rarely, we must go ahead with the module launch. Moreover, he says that the module must be delivered on time; otherwise, the delay will have a very poor impact on the future of the Indian development centre of the firm.

Questions

1. What are the various dilemmas in the above case?
2. What are the various options available? Which one will you choose and why?

CASE STUDY: 72

You are the district officer of a large city. Because of greater opportunities for employment and sources of living, lot of people from the rural areas comes to this city to work as daily-wage labourers. They have set up temporary tents and slums in the outskirts of the city and have been living so for 8 to 10 years, with their families. Recently, the state government has taken a decision to launch metro services in the city, and the land on city's outskirts (including the tents and slums) has to be cleared to make way for a metro station. You have been asked to start an anti-encroachment drive to clear this land of tents and slums. But you also know that such a move will leave these poor people and their family homeless.

Question

1. What will you do? Evaluate the below options, with merits and demerits:
   (a) Write to Chief Secretary, asking him to stop the plan of launching a metro in the city.
   (b) Ask the slum-dwellers to go back to the villages and try to earn a living there.
   (c) Ask your superiors for guidance.
   (d) Ask your sub-ordinate officers to take charge of the demolition drive and thus delegate the responsibility to your juniors.

CASE STUDY: 73

You are posted as the Superintendent of Police of a district infamous for robbery and extortions. One day, during your morning walk, you notice that a group of people is mercilessly beating up an alleged extortionist whom they apprehended from their neighbourhood. Since you are not in police uniform, the mob does not recognize you and continue to beat the accused. When you question the mob that why are they not taking the culprit to the police station, they say that they are fed up with the slow judicial process of the country and are sure that once taken to police station, the culprit will be soon out on bail and will again start engaging in robbery and extortion.

Questions

1. What will be your immediate reaction in this situation?
2. In long term, how will you make sure that justice-delivery in your district is speeded up?

CASE STUDY: 74

You are the Civil Surgeon of a backward district, which is recently seeing a lot of dengue cases. More than 20 children have died so far in the district hospital, and the situation is very grim. Families of the patients are complaining that there are insufficient beds in the hospital, because of which they are being denied admission. They allege that the attitude of the doctors and medical staff is also very rude towards the patients. You have issued a directive to the doctors and staff to cancel their leaves and be present in the hospital at all times. However, the medical staff and doctors are complaining that they are being overworked and that they need adequate rest to perform at their best. The doctors are threatening to go on a strike if they are forced to work for long hours.

Questions

1. Do you think that in professions like medicine, doctors should be allowed to go on strike?
2. How will you tackle this situation?
3. What are the options available to you? Evaluate each of them, with merits and demerits.

CASE STUDY: 75

You are an evaluating officer with Mid-Day Meal (MDM) programme. You made a visit to a government school to evaluate the mid-meal service in the school. The mid-day meal was being received from centralized kitchen and was being served to the children during mid-morning break. Children who brought their own lunch from home were not interested in taking the meal. Children who didn't bring lunch had no other option but to take the mid-day meal. You noticed that children were not enthusiastic about taking the food. They were just taking it out of obligation. They were not enjoying the food and some of them were even wasting it. The school authorities offered you to taste the food and you did the same. You found the taste of the food as bad and not delectable. Looking at the amount of money being put in the scheme and the manpower employed to facilitate the service you feel it's going in waste since children are not enjoying it as it is meant for them only.

The mid-day meal menu is planned keeping in mind the nutritional requirements of children. A variety of dishes are served through MDM. The objective of MDM is to improve school retention among children. In spite of planning this scheme by giving importance to all the aspects, it fails to meet its goal.

Question

1. In this scenario, what will you do on your part to find a solution to the above problem?

CASE STUDY: 76

You are a District Child Protection Officer and Head of The District Labour Committee for Child Protection under Integrated Child Protection Scheme (ICPS) Of Govt. of India, Implemented by State Government through Child Care Institutions (CCIs). CCIs are funded by the Government and meant for the children who are either orphan or left to be on their own. Major Job of these institutions is to provide care and protection to these children and act as their guardians. You make a visit to one of these institutions to collect data for an ongoing project. As part of the project, you interact with both the children and various stakeholders of these CCIs. During your interaction with children, they disclose to you that the authorities are physically abusing them severely. The children wanted something to be done in this regard, but at the same time they were scared of authorities and they did not want them to find out that they have complained about them. Children expressed their hope in you and you also want to help them.

Question

1. By keeping the children's interest and safety in view, how will you handle the situation?

CASE STUDY: 77

You are posted as a Director, Social Welfare Department of State Govt. Being head of the department, you are getting many complaints against Child Development project Officer (CDPO) who is a drawing and disbursing officer/Head of Office for the ICDS project under your control. CDPO is engaging in corrupt practices like taking commission from suppliers of supplementary nutrition for children at Anganwadi centres. CDPO is making money, and she does not hesitate to compromise with quality and quantity of supplementary nutrition. You talk to this officer many times to stop such malpractices, but she does not change her mind. You are scared to complain about her as she has a good nexus with higher authorities. You are also afraid of her as complaining about her can hamper your promotion which you deserve and is due shortly, given the number of years of experience you hold.

Questions

1. In such a situation, what action is required on your part?
2. What steps are required to run the supplementary nutrition program smoothly?

CASE STUDY: 78

You are working as a District Protection Officer under Protection of Women against Domestic Violence Act. The domestic help working in your house faces violence at the hands of her sister-in-law and her husband. She shares the same residential facility with them. They also put some false allegations against her elder son (aged 15 years). When she complains about them to the elders of her family, they do not support her. Instead, they believe in what her sister-in-law and her husband say. She also files a police complaint against them, but the police also do not believe her.

Her husband is not in a condition to make a living for the family or to look after his children, as he does not keep well. She has no choice but to work in different houses to earn a living and leave her two children at home under the care of same family members who did not support her. She is scared that they may also physically abuse her children in her absence.

Question

1. In the above situation, how will you help your domestic help to get justice?

CASE STUDY: 79

You are a teacher in a school. You notice that one of the female students of your class is behaving differently. She has become quite, inattentive in class, looks outside through window and her grades in exams are also going down. You decide to talk to her. However, she does not disclose anything to you but you doubt that something is definitely wrong with her. After trying for a number of times, you win her confidence and she shares that her grandfather has been sexually abusing her. Her parents were employed and after school she was under the care of her grandfather. In her parent's absence, her grandfather abused her and also threatened her not to disclose to anyone. You want to bring the matter into the knowledge of her parents, but you are scared for the child. You do not want her to go through the same ordeal of narrating the story to her parents and loose her confidence as she was excellent in her studies, but this incident has left a mark in her life. Grandfather is a close family member, and the situation might take an ugly turn in house, which might further traumatize the child. You want the parents to believe in you and not involve the child too much.

Questions

1. In the above situation, what are the options available before you?
2. What will you do to get the confidence of the child back?

CASE STUDY: 80

In villages of a tribal development block in the district where you are posted as D.C., local administration has taken all the grazing land of villagers for social forestry programme. As a result, animal husbandry has reduced to a great extent. As money making mono culture trees were planted in the grazing land to meet out the requirement of industries, it was not considered fruitful. Consequently, the villagers opposed it. In spite of consensus, local administration wanted to maintain the status quo. As a result, the opposition was on the increase. Villagers started taking out sapling to destroy the plantation. On account of this, villagers were arrested by the police daily. The Block Development Officer (BDO) tries his best but failed as the matter was a policy-related one. The decision in this regard was still awaited. The administration as well as villagers continued destroying the plantation, administration found itself helpless and the matter is lying with you.

Questions

1. Since the grazing land is not in use, what immediate action is required?
2. What will be your role in solving the case?
3. What action do you suggest for promoting social forestry programme in the district?

CASE STUDY: 81

A high school girl of 15 years was promised a job by a friendly uncle of her town. The girl left her home with this uncle. On the way, the uncle repeatedly assaulted her sexually and sold her to a brothel. One day there was a raid on that brothel. She was rescued and sent to a shelter home run by an NGO in the partnership of Child Welfare Department of State Government under Integrated Child Protection Scheme (ICPS). The role of this shelter home was to provide the girl and other such girls' specialized medical care and schooling and happiness in life. But she was sexually assaulted by the in-charge of the shelter home like other girls and was threatened not to tell anybody about this. The abuse at the shelter home came to light after an employee telephoned Child line. The children were rescued and the in-charge of the shelter home was arrested by the police.

The girl and other children were presented before the District Child Welfare Committee under ICPS as per Juvenile Justice Act to decide how and where they should be looked after. The Child Welfare Committee sent them to a Children Home run by Child Welfare Department of State Government.

Once again the girl landed in another abusive situation just after three months in the Children Home. One day an investigation team discovered the girl and six other girls had complained of being sexually abused by the caretaker, and other staff members of the Home resorted to physical abuse and torture. The similar situation is prevailing in most of the Child Care Institutions under Child Welfare Department of State Government headed by you.

Questions

1. In such situations, being the head of the department, what will be your role in ultimate rehabilitation of the girl and other such girls living in Children's Homes/Shelte Homes?
2. What strategy will you adopt to ensure the proper implementation of POCSO Act and Juvenile Justice Act in the Child Care Institutions under your control?

CASE STUDY: 82

Recently you are posted as Block Development Officer in a far-flung Tribal Developmen Block. You found that tribal forest villagers are facing many problems due to illega activities such as:

1. Commercial dealings between the local forest administration and the owners o Tile factories. A dozen of forest villages have become labour camps of the fores department. The villagers have been deprived not only of the wood for agricultura instruments but of firewood also. On the other hand, more than a thousand quinta of wood is burnt daily in the ovens of the tile factories located in the forest area. The wood consumption in these factories is increasing day by day and became so high tha it cannot be fulfilled by legal means. Thus, illegal cutting of trees with the help of loca forest administration is going on. Illegal wood stocks in huge quantity can be seen in these factories.
2. Similarly, illegal mining of soil in this area has become a big problem. The tile factories get clay for making kilns by illegal mining of soil in these forest villages with the help of local mines department. As per rule, pits should not be deeper than 10 feet, but 20 feet deep pits can be seen in this forest area. When the soil is removed from the roots of trees, either they fall down or they dry up. During the last 10 years wherever fores land has been dug up, pits can still be seen, where even grass doesn't grow.
3. Huge amount has been spent on various welfare plans/schemes for tribal villagers but the people concerned have not benefited from these plans. These villagers were given loans for agricultural equipment, digging of wells, construction of houses, etc It is found that those who could obtain loan for oxen did not get it for carts and those who had carts did not get loan for oxen. Loan could never be obtained on time, because of the delaying tactics of the officials. This loan was given through rural banks. The thumb impressions of the illiterate villagers were taken on the blank papers, withou telling them the cause. They came to know about the consequences only when the concerned official visited their houses for the recovery of the instalments.

   By giving full exemption to these tribal villagers on gobar gas plants, about 150 families have been provided with this facility, out of which more than 100 families did not have sufficient gobar (cow dung) and those had sufficient cow dung were not given this facility.
4. Under the Tribal Housing Scheme for the landless and homeless tribes, 10 families of a village were given 15×10 feet plot each of which was quite insufficient for the family

and their cattle. For this reason, plot has been covered by wooden huts. A few non-tribal influential people of these villages took the benefit in the name of these tribal, completing the formalities in collusion with the local administration.

5. Villages have school buildings but without students. On paper there are schools for these villages but without teachers.
6. These tribal villagers are not comfortable and found themselves unfitted in the existing model of development. Their social values and concepts of development are quite different from nontribes, but they are treated in the same way.

Questions

1. Would it be possible for you to look into the linkages of their concepts of development with their needs and quality of life?
2. If yes, what kind of action plan is required?
3. What direct action would you take on your part to resolve the problems?

CASE STUDY: 83

Mr. Manoj Kumar is recently appointed as the Chairman of Tobacco Board. He is a very sincere and committed officer. Also, previously he has held various high-level positions.

Tobacco is an important commercial crop grown in India. It occupies the third position in the world with an annual production of about 800 million kg Tobacco and tobacco products earn approximately ₹ 20,000 crores to the national exchequer by way of excise duty, and approximately ₹ 5,000 crores by way of foreign exchange every year. But recently, the tobacco production in some parts of the country suffered from setback. Farmers and farm-labourers committed suicide because of crop failures and mounting debt. Also the farmers have gone for strikes and dharnas against economic policies of the Government.

Mr. Kumar has a very close relative who stays in Canada. He has always shown his presence in almost every functions of this particular relative. He does not have an attitude to say 'NO' to his family members and relatives.

Recently, he got a call from Canada to attend a marriage party of this particular relative there. But, amidst the ongoing suicide crisis of farmers and related agitations in the country, he fled to Canada to attend his relative's marriage.

Questions

1. Do you think Mr. Kumar is a responsible officer? Justify your viewpoint.
2. What you would have done if you were in place of Mr. Kumar?

CASE STUDY: 84

Mr. Ashok Kumar is the Deputy Superintendent of Police (DSP) of the Prohibition Enforcement Wing in a State. He has a very close childhood friend, named Naresh, who has now become a red sanders logs smuggler. Both are still good friends.

DSP led a four-member team to track down a prohibition offender and his associates. Mr. Kumar and his team seized around 4,000 litres of rectified spirit and confiscated a van during the raid recently. But the notorious bootlegger and his associates managed to escape.

DSP, however, instigated by Naresh, led the team comprising of the same four officers and raided a poultry farm. Naresh had given ₹ 3.5 crore worth of red sanders logs to owner of the poultry firm, and he was refusing to pay for it or return it.

Upon finding a huge haul of red sanders logs, the DSP told the four policemen that he must inform the appropriate authorities to take further course of action against the owner of the poultry firm. He also told the policemen to wait inside the police vehicle.

They were not aware that DSP has already informed Naresh about this raid. After the DSP and his team left the farm, Naresh and his men, who were waiting outside the farm, took the logs away.

Questions

1. Does Mr. Kumar's action reflect the integrity of the public office he holds?
2. How should Mr. Kumar have dealt with Naresh?

CASE STUDY: 85

You are the academic dean of a reputed college. You have recently received complaints from many parents that one of the senior professors is very rude to the students, and even resorts to severe physical punishments. The professor in question is a highly regarded academician with excellent teaching record and has won numerous awards, including the President's Award for Excellence in Teaching. When you confront the professor, he admits, but says that he feels punishment is necessary to make students focus on studies.

Questions

1. Evaluate each of the below options available to you:
   (a) Ask the professor for resignation.
   (b) Go to the students and tell them that professors need to be strict with them for the good of the students.
   (c) Transfer the professor to another department.
   (d) Resign yourself from the position of dean.
2. Also mention any other option which you have, and which one will you choose, with justification.

CASE STUDY: 86

You are the in-charge of the office that supervises the allotment of official residences to the incumbent Members of Parliament (MPs). You are finding it very challenging to issue allotment for all MPs because there is a crunch of appropriate bungalows. In the meanwhile, it has been brought to your notice that some of the ex-MPs are not vacating the official residences allotted to them, even after they are no longer entitled for the same. Numerous notices have been served to these ex-MPs, but there has been no response. Some of these ex-MPs are very influential and one of them has even threatened your office not to bother him with notices—he plans to stay in his residence for at least 2 years. Meanwhile, incumbent MPs are quickly demanding allocation of official residences.

Questions

1. Evaluate the below options:
   (a) Forcibly evict the erring ex-MPs.
   (b) Approach your superiors and ask for guidance.
   (c) Send a final notice to all the ex-MPs regarding the dates by which the residences have to be vacated and the charges that would be levied after such last date.
2. Also mention any other option that you have. Which option will you choose? Give justifications.

CASE STUDY: 87

You have recently been promoted as an Executive Engineer of a state road construction department, and the first assignment is construction of an all-weather road in a district, which connects a big but remote village to the state highway. There is an old dirt road that exists and is to be replaced by the new, broader road. During your inspection on site, you find that there is encroachment on either side of the road. Many villagers have built their house and business on the government land meant for the road. When you discuss this issue with the local Gram Panchayat, they understand the issue involved, but reject any proposal for demolition of the illegal contractions on the road.

Questions

1. What precautions should you take before you start the project and why?
2. What are the problems you anticipate and how do you plan to address them?

CASE STUDY: 88

You are the District Development officer of a drought-prone district. As a part of your responsibilities, you are required to send a report to the Chief Secretary of the state, declaring whether your district is affected by drought or not, and if yes, the extent of drought in the district. Only then is the compensation released for the affected people. For the past few years, your district has been drought-affected. However, this year, most areas in your district have received sufficient rainfall and you want to send an accurate report to the Chief Secretary. The MLA of your district, however, has asked you to send a report which declares the district as drought-affected, so that the compensation so received can be utilized in other development programmes which are facing funds shortage. The

Tehsildars and the Sub-Divisional Magistrate are not sure whether conditions in the district can be rightly classified as drought-affected.

Questions

1. What are the ethical and moral dilemmas in this case?
2. What are the options available to you? Identify the merits and demerits of each and choose the best option, with justifications.

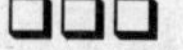

APPENDICES

Right to Public Services Legislation in India

1 APPENDIX

Right to Public Services legislation in India comprises statutory laws which guarantee time bound delivery of services for various public services rendered by the Government to citizen and provides mechanism for punishing the errant public servant who is deficient in providing the service stipulated under the statute. Right to Service legislation are meant to reduce corruption among the government officials and to increase transparency and public accountability. Madhya Pradesh became the first state in India to enact Right to Service Act on 18 August 2010 and Bihar was the second to enact this bill on 25 July 2011. Several other states like Bihar, Delhi, Punjab, Rajasthan, Himachal Pradesh, Kerala, Uttarakhand, Haryana, Uttar Pradesh, Odisha and Jharkhand have introduced similar legislation for effectuating the right to service to the citizen.

Framework

The common framework of the legislations in various states includes, granting of "right to public services", which are to be provided to the public by the designated official within the stipulated time frame. The public services which are to be granted as a right under the legislations are generally notified separately through Gazette notification. Some of the common public services which are to be provided within the fixed time frame as a right under the Acts, includes issuing caste, birth, marriage and domicile certificates, electric connections, voter's card, ration cards, copies of land records, etc.

On failure to provide the service by the designated officer within the given time or rejected to provide the service, the aggrieved person can approach the First Appellate Authority. The First Appellate Authority, after making a hearing, can accept or reject the appeal by making a written order stating the reasons for the order and intimate the same to the applicant, and can order the public servant to provide the service to the applicant.

An appeal can be made from the order of the First Appellate Authority to the Second Appellate Authority, who can either accept or reject the application, by making a written order stating the reasons for the order and intimate the same to the applicant, and can order the public servant to provide the service to the applicant or can impose penalty on the designated officer for deficiency of service without any reasonable cause, which can range from ₹ 500 to ₹ 5000 or may recommend disciplinary proceedings. The applicant may be compensated out of the penalty imposed on the officer. The appellate authorities has been granted certain powers of a Civil Court while trying a suit under Code of Civil Procedure, 1908, like production of documents and issuance of summon to the Designated officers and appellants.

Implementing states

State	Act title	Status
Punjab	Right to Public Service Act, 2011	Notified
Uttarakhand	The Uttarakhand Right to Service Act, 2011	Notified
Madhya Pradesh	Madhya Pradesh Lok Sewaon Ke Pradan Ki Guarantee Adhiniyam, 2010	Enacted
Bihar	Bihar Lok Sewaon Ka Adhikar Adhiniyam, 2011	Enacted
Delhi	Delhi (Right of Citizen to Time Bound Delivery of Services) Act, 2011	Notified
Jharkhand	Right to Service Act, 2011	Notified
Himachal Pradesh	Himachal Pradesh Public Services Guarantee Act, 2011	Notified
Rajasthan	Rajasthan Public Service Guarantee Act, 2011	Notified
Uttar Pradesh	Janhit Guarantee Act, 2011	Enacted
Kerala	The Kerala State Right to Service Act, 2012	Enacted
Karnataka	The Karnataka (Right of Citizens to Time Bound Delivery of Services) Bill, 2011	Notified
Chhattisgarh	Chhattisgarh Lok Seva Guarantee Bill, 2011	Notified
Jammu and Kashmir	The Jammu and Kashmir Public Services Guarantee Act, 2011	Notified
Odisha	Odisha Right to Public Services Act, 2012	Notified
Assam	Assam Right to Public Services Act, 2012	Notified
Central Government	Citizen's Charter and Grievance Redressal Bill 2011	Proposed
Gujarat	Gujarat (Right of Citizens to Public Services) Bill, 2013	Enacted
West Bengal	West Bengal Right to Public Services Bill, 2013	Notified
Goa	The Goa (Right to Time-Bound Delivery of Public Services) Act, 2013	Notified
Haryana	The Haryana Right to Service Act, 2014	Notified
Maharashtra	Maharashtra Right to Public Services Ordinance, 2015	Notified

❑❑❑

The Right of Citizens for Time Bound Delivery of Goods and Services and Redressal of Their Grievances Bill, 2011

2 APPENDIX

The Bill was introduced in the Lok Sabha on 20 December 2011. The Bill was referred to the Department Related Standing Committee on Personnel, Public Grievances, Law and Justice (Chairperson: Mr. Shantaram Naik). The Report was submitted on 30 August 2012.

AIMS OF THE BILL

- The Bill seeks to create a mechanism to ensure timely delivery of goods and services to citizens.
- Every public authority is required to publish a citizens charter within six months of the commencement of the Act. The Charter will detail the goods and services to be provided and their timelines for delivery.
- A citizen may file a complaint regarding any grievance related to: (a) citizens charter; (b) functioning of a public authority; or (c) violation of a law, policy or scheme.
- The Bill requires all public authorities to appoint officers to redress grievances. Grievances are to be redressed within 30 working days. The Bill also provides for the appointment of Central and State Public Grievance Redressal Commissions.
- A penalty of up to ₹ 50,000 may be levied upon the responsible officer or the Grievance Redressal Officer for failure to render services.

KEY POINTS

- Parliament may not have the jurisdiction to regulate the functioning of state public officials as state public services fall within the purview of state legislatures.
- This Bill may create a parallel grievance redressal mechanism as many central and state laws have established similar mechanisms.
- Companies that render services under a statutory obligation or a licence may be required to publish citizens charters and provide a grievance redressal mechanism.
- The Commissioners may be removed without a judicial inquiry on an allegation of misbehaviour or incapacity. This differs from the procedure under other legislations.

- Appeals from the Commissions' decisions on matters of corruption will lie before the Lokpal or Lokayukta. The Lokpal and some Lokayukta have not been established.
- Only citizens can seek redressal of grievances under the Bill. The Bill does not enable foreign nationals who also use services such as driving licenses, electricity, etc., to file complaints.

PART A: HIGHLIGHTS OF THE BILL

Context

The Bill refers to a 'citizens charter' which is a document that defines the standard of services to be provided by an entity. The citizens charter will also provide the time frame within which goods and services are to be provided. The concept of citizens charter was introduced in the United Kingdom in 1991 and subsequently was adopted by various countries such as Belgium (1992), Malaysia (1993) and Australia (1997).

In 1997, at a chief ministers' conference, an Action Plan was approved requiring the central and state governments to formulate citizens charters for enterprises with a large public interface. In 2007, the Second Administrative Reforms Commission recommended that citizens charters should stipulate penalties for non- compliance. In 2008, the Standing Committee on Personnel, Public Grievances, Law and Justice recommended giving statutory status to grievance redressal mechanisms. The Central Information Commission also recommended that grievance redressal systems should be strengthened to reduce the use of the Right to Information Act, 2005 to redress grievances.

The President, in her address to Parliament in June 2009, had stated that the government would focus on ensuring effective delivery of public services. The Standing Committee that had examined the Lokpal Bill, 2011 recommended the creation of a separate legislation to deal with citizens charter and grievance redressal. The Parliament on 27 August 2011 while adopting the 'Sense of the House' Resolution on Lokpal, agreed in principle to the establishment of a citizens charter.

Currently, government departments deal with grievances internally. Persons may also approach the High Court through writ petitions. As of January 2011, 131 citizens charters were finalized by the central government departments and 729 citizens charters were finalized by state government departments. Additionally, by March 2012, several states had enacted laws providing for grievance redressal mechanisms.

KEY FEATURES

The Bill requires public authorities to publish a citizens charter within six months of enactment of the Bill. The charter should specify the services and the quality of services to be provided by the public authority. The head of departments are responsible for disseminating and updating the citizens charter.

Public Authority

- Public authorities include: (a) constitutional and statutory authorities; (b) entities established under a notification; and (c) public-private partnerships. They also include NGOs that are substantially government funded, government companies, and companies that provide services under a licence or a statutory obligation.

- Public authorities are required to establish Information Facilitation Centres for efficient and effective delivery of services and redressal of grievances. Information Facilitation Centres may include customer care centres, call centres, help desks and people's support centres.

Public Grievance Redressal Commissions

- The Bill establishes Central and State Grievance Redressal Commissions. Each Commission would consist of a Chief Commissioner and up to 10 Commissioners. The Commissioners would be appointed by the President (Governor) on the recommendation of a selection committee. This committee would consist of the Prime Minister (Chief Minister), the Leader of the Opposition in the Lok Sabha (Legislative Assembly) and a sitting Supreme Court (High Court) judge.
- The Commissioners should be: (a) present or former Secretaries to the central (state) government; or (b) present or former Supreme Court judges or Chief Justices of a High Court (district court judges for 10 years, or High Court judges); or (c) eminent persons with at least 20 years (15 years) of experience in social sectors with a postgraduate degree in a relevant sector. The Commissioners may be removed by an order of the President (Governor) under certain conditions.

COMPLAINT MECHANISM

- ***Complaint***: Any citizen may file a complaint for (a) failure in delivery of goods or services listed in the citizens charter; (b) the functioning of the public authority; and (c) any violation of a law, policy, programme, order or scheme. Complaints have to be redressed within 30 working days.
- Complaints have to be made to the Grievance Redressal Officer (GRO). GROs are to be appointed by each public authority at the central, state, district, sub-district, municipality and panchayat levels. The GRO is required to: (a) ensure that grievances are redressed within 30 working days; (b) ensure that disciplinary action is taken against a defaulting officer if he has acted negligently; and (c) recommend penalties and compensation where an individual has wilfully neglected to deliver services or there is a prima facie ground for a case under the Prevention of Corruption Act, 1988. The GRO has to inform the complainant about the action taken on the complaint.
- ***Appeal***: The orders of the GRO may be appealed before the Designated Authority (DA). The DA shall be an officer above the rank of the GRO and outside the concerned public authority. (According to a statement made by the Minister of State for Personnel, Public Grievances and Pensions, the DA shall be an officer at the district level. The DA shall dispose of appeals within 30 working days of their receipt. If a complaint with the GRO is not redressed within 30 working days, the GRO has to forward it as an appeal to the DA. The DA may penalize the defaulting officers.
- ***Second Appeal***: The DA's orders may be appealed before the Central or State Public Grievance Redressal Commission within 30 working days. Appeals relating to

complaints arising out of functioning of the central (state) departments would lie before the Central (State) Commission. The Commissions have to dispose of the appeal within 60 working days.

- ***Third Appeal***: In relation to an offence under the Prevention of Corruption Act, 1988, an appeal against the decision of the Commissions shall lie with the Lokpal or the Lokayukta.
- ***Suo moto mechanism***: The Central and State Commissions can *suo moto* refer matters related to non- delivery of goods and services to the heads of government departments. The Commissions may also initiate *suo moto* inquiry if they believe that there are reasonable grounds to inquire into the matter.
- Complaints may also be made to the Commissions in certain cases. It is the duty of the Commissions to inquire into complaints by persons: (a) who are unable to file appeals before the DA; (b) who are refused redress of grievances; (c) whose complaints are not disposed of within 30 days; and (d) who are denied access to the citizens charter because it has not been prepared or has not been widely disseminated.

Penalties

- **GRO:** The Bill requires the GRO to recommend penalties to the DA when: (a) he is convinced that the default was due to wilful neglect by an officer; or (b) when there is prima facie evidence of corruption.
- **DA and Commissions:** The Bill empowers the DA and the Commissions to impose a maximum penalty of ₹ 50,000 upon the defaulting officer and the GRO. Penalties may be imposed upon the defaulting officer when he has acted in a mala fide manner or has failed to discharge his responsibility in a proper manner.

A portion of the penalty may be awarded as compensation to the complainant.

- If there is evidence of corruption against the defaulting officer, the DA and the Commissions would have to refer the matter to appropriate authorities. Additionally, the DA may initiate proceedings in such cases.
- Disciplinary proceedings may be initiated by the GRO, DA and the Commissions against the defaulting officer if there is evidence of mala fide action.
- In any appeal proceeding, where it is alleged that the grievance has not been redressed by the GRO, the burden of proof shall be on the GRO.

PART B: KEY ISSUES AND ANALYSIS

Parliament's Jurisdiction to Regulate State Public Officials

The Bill regulates the functioning of departments and public officials at the central and state level. It also establishes Commissions at the central and state level. 'State public services; State Public Service Commission' is included in the State List (Entry 41) of the Seventh Schedule of the Constitution. This implies that the power to make laws to regulate the functioning of state public officials lies solely with state legislatures. Thus, Parliament may not have jurisdiction to enact laws governing such services and officials.

In this regard, the Ministry has stated that the provisions of the Bill relate to 'actionable wrongs' which comes under the concurrent list. This view was accepted by the Standing Committee.

The Supreme Court has held that, "Wrong means an actionable wrong and it must consist of: (a) an act or omission amounting to an infringement of a legal right of a person or a breach of legal duty towards him; and (b) the act or omission must have caused harm or damage to that person in some way, the damage being either actual or presumed". Under the Bill, complaints may be filed for violation of any policy or scheme. The claims under these schemes and policies may be non-justiciable (unenforceable by courts). It is unclear whether schemes and policies which are not justiciable would fall under the meaning of 'actionable wrong'.

Several states such as Delhi, Punjab and Bihar have also enacted their own grievance redressal laws. The mechanism provided under these laws is different from that provided under the Bill.

Lack of Clarity on the Meaning of Public Authority

Clause 2(n)

It is not clear whether the Bill applies to private entities only if they are established or constituted under a notification. The term 'public authorities' has been defined broadly to mean authorities constituted under: (a) the Constitution or under any central or state law; (b) an agreement between the government and a private entity as a PPP; and (c) any entity established under a notification or order of the government. This definition also includes: (i) non-governmental organizations that receive government finances either directly or indirectly, and (ii) other companies that are supplying goods or services to fulfil a statutory obligation, or under a license or authorization by law. It is not clear if these organizations are required to be established under a notification.

It is pertinent to note that the Right to Information Act, 2005 includes private entities as long as they are controlled or financed by the government. Private sector companies are covered by other laws such as Consumer Protection Act, 1986 and the Competition Act, 2002. Inclusion under this Bill may lead to multiple dispute settlement forums being available for the same dispute. For instance, grievances related to services to be provided under a contract would fall under the Consumer Protection Act and this Bill.

Multiplicity of Grievance Redressal Forums

Clause 2(f)

This Bill provides grievance redressal under several circumstances including violation of any law, policy or scheme. Some existing and proposed laws provide their own grievance redressal mechanisms, for instance, the Mahatma Gandhi National Rural Employment Guarantee Act, 2005, Right of Children to Free and Compulsory Education, 2009, National Food Security Bill, 2011, and the Public Procurement Bill, 2012.

There could be an overlap of jurisdictions in some cases, as grievances under these legislations may be covered under this Bill as well. It is unclear as to which mechanism may be approached first, and whether seeking relief under one law bars remedies under the other.

Furthermore, the commissions established under these legislations are specialized in nature. They comprise persons of eminence in the field to which the laws relate. For instance, commissions under the National Food Security Bill, 2011 comprise persons with experience in the field of food security, agriculture and health.

Exclusion of non-citizens

Clause 2(f)

A complaint may only be filed by a citizen. However, certain services may be used by both citizens and foreign nationals. For example, a foreign national is eligible to apply for a driving license under Indian law. The rationale for excluding foreign nationals from the purview of the redressal mechanism is unclear.

Under some state laws, the criterion for accessing grievance redressal mechanism is the eligibility of the complainant and not his citizenship. The Punjab Right to Services Act, 2011 and the Rajasthan Guaranteed Delivery of Public Services Act, 2011 provide access to the redressal mechanism to all 'eligible persons'. Under these Acts an 'eligible person' is defined as 'any person who is eligible for the notified services'. The Standing Committee has recommended that the Ministry review whether non-citizens can be brought under the Bill.

Inconsistencies in the Appeals Procedure

Clause 47, 28 and 44

Under the Bill, if the Commission is satisfied that a prima facie case of corruption exists, it will refer the matter to the 'appropriate authority'. The Bill also provides that the Commissions' decisions related to corruption may be appealed before the Lokpal or the Lokayukta. This raises three issues.

First, under the Bill, the Commission is not empowered to adjudicate matters related to corruption. It is only empowered to refer the matter to the appropriate authority. It is unclear how an appeal may be made before the Lokpal or the Lokayukta in the absence of the Commissions' power to decide on cases of corruption.

Second, the Bill does not provide a process to appeal against the Commissions' orders that do not relate to corruption. Third, the Lokpal is yet to be instituted at the centre and a number of states have not yet established Lokayukta.

The Standing Committee has recommended that appeals to the Lokpal and Lokayukta should not be provided. It observed that the Lokpal and Lokayukta are anti-corruption agencies, whereas, the Bill addresses the issue of delivery of services. It also noted that the Bill already provided for three levels of appeal, and that a fourth appeal to the Lokpal or the Lokayukta is not required.

Removal of Members of the Central and State Grievance Commissions

Clause 20 and 37

Members of the Commissions can be removed by an order of the President or the Governor. The Bill states that the government may by rules regulate the investigation procedure for removal of the Commissioners for misbehaviour or incapacity. However, it does not require a judicial inquiry to be conducted in case there is an allegation of misbehaviour (acquisition of financial or such other interest) or incapacity of the Commissioners.

This is different from the process provided under some legislations. For example, the Competition Act, 2002, the Right to Information Act, 2005 and the Protection of Human Rights Act, 1993 require a judicial inquiry to be conducted before removal of the Commissioners when there is an allegation of misbehaviour or incapacity against them. The Electronic Delivery of Services Bill, 2011 and the Lokpal and Lokayukta Bill, 2011 also have a similar inquiry procedure.

Inconsistency between the Powers of the DA and the Commissions

Clause 11(10) and 28

The Bill provides for two levels of appeals by a complainant: first to the DA, and then to the Commission. There is an inconsistency between the powers of the two. If there is a prima facie indication of corruption, the DA may either refer the matter to the appropriate authority or initiate proceedings. However, if the complainant appeals against the DA's decision to the Commission, it can only refer the matter to the appropriate authority. Unlike the DA, the Commission does not have the power to initiate proceedings.

India's Citizen's Charter and Grievance Redressal Bill, 2011

3 APPENDIX

The Citizen's Charter and Grievance Redressal Bill, 2011 in India is also known as The Right of Citizens for Time Bound Delivery of Goods and Services and Redressal of their Grievances Bill, 2011 or Citizens Charter Bill. It was tabled by V. Narayanasamy, Minister of State for Personnel, Public Grievances and Pensions, in Lok Sabha in December 2011.

The Bill seeks to confer on every citizen the right to time-bound delivery of specified goods and services and to provide a mechanism for grievance redressal. The Bill makes it mandatory for every public authority to publish a Citizen's Charter within six months of the commencement of the Act, failing which the official concerned would face action, including a fine of up to ₹ 50,000 from his salary and disciplinary proceedings.

The bill came after Anna Hazare asked for its provisions to be included in the Jan Lokpal Bill.

JAN LOKPAL BILL

The Jan Lokpal Bill, also referred to as the Citizen's Ombudsman Bill, is an anti-corruption bill drafted and drawn up by civil society activists in India seeking the appointment of a Jan Lokpal, an independent body to investigate corruption cases. This bill also proposes improvements to the Lokpal and Lokayukta Bill 2011, which was to be passed by Lok Sabha in December 2011. The Jan Lokpal Bill aims to effectively deter corruption, compensate citizen grievances and protect whistle-blowers. The prefix *Jan* (translation: citizens) signifies that these improvements include inputs provided by "ordinary citizens" through an activist-driven, non-governmental public consultation.

The word *Lokpal' was coined in 1963 by L.M. Singhvi, a Member of Parliament during a debate mechanisms. His son Dr. was head of the Parliament reviewing the bill but later resigned from the post after a sex-tape controversy.* In order to draw the attention of the government, a focused campaign "India Against Corruption" (IAC) was started in 2011. Anna Hazare is the head of civil society and the IAC movement, being a foreground for Jan Lokpal campaign. Through these collaborative efforts till August 2011, IAC was able to upload the 23rd version of the Jan Lokpal Bill draft.

Lokpal Bill

The Lokpal Bill was first introduced by Shanti Bhushan in 1968 and passed the 4th Lok Sabha in 1969. But before it could be passed by Rajya Sabha, the Lok Sabha was dissolved and the bill lapsed. Subsequent versions were re-introduced in 1971, 1977, 1985, 1989, 1996, 1998, 2001, 2005 and in 2008, but none of them were passed. In 2011, during the Parliament's Winter Session, the Lok Sabha passed the controversial Lokpal Bill, but could not be passed by Rajya Sabha due to shortage of time in the winter session of 2011. Government has not put Lokpal bill again in Rajya Sabha.

Timeline and cost

The Lokpal Bill has been introduced in the Parliament a total of eight times since 1968.

- 1968 – 3 lakh (300,000)
- 1971 – 20 lakh (2 million)
- 1977 – 25 lakh (2.5 million)
- 1985 – 25 lakh
- 1989 – 35 lakh (3.5 million) – PM under Lokpal
- 1996 – 1 crore (10 million) – PM under Lokpal
- 2001 – 35 crore (350 million) – PM under Lokpal
- 2011 – 1700 crore (17 billion)
- 2012 – 2000 crore (20 billion)

Current Anti-Corruption Laws and Organizations

While India currently has a number of laws intended to stem corruption, supporters of the Jan Lokpal Bill have argued that the current laws are inadequate in light of the large number and size of scandals in India.

Central Vigilance Commission (CVC)

CVC has a staff strength of between 200 and 250 employees. If one went by international standards, India needs 28 anti-corruption staff in CVC to check corruption of 57 lakh employees. There has been considerable delay in many cases for grant of sanction for prosecution against corrupt government officials. The permission to prosecute such officials acts as a deterrent in the drive to eradicate corruption and bring transparency in the system.

Central Bureau of Investigation (CBI)

Because the CBI is under the control of the central government, it needs a go-ahead from central agencies to initiate criminal proceedings. By then, the accused can take advantage of such a situation. He can get time to pressure the complainant and intimidate him so that the case be withdrawn. In the Jan Lokpal Bill, it is proposed that both of these wings be merged into the Lokpal. This would enable the Lokpal to be completely independent of the government and free from ministerial influence in its investigations.

Inspiration

The bill was inspired by the Hong Kong Independent Commission Against Corruption (ICAC). In the 1970s, the level of corruption in Hong Kong was seen so high, that the government created the commission with direct powers to investigate and deal with corruption. In the first instance, the ICAC sacked 119 out of 180 police officers.

Key Features of Proposed Bill

Some important features of the proposed bill are:

1. To establish a central government anti-corruption institution called *Lokpal*, supported by *Lokayukta* at the state level.
2. As is the case with the Supreme Court of India and Cabinet Secretariat, the *Lokpal* will be supervised by the Cabinet Secretary and the Election Commission. As a result, it will be completely independent of the government and free from ministerial influence in its investigations.
3. Members will be appointed by judges, Indian Administrative Service officers with a clean record, private citizens and constitutional authorities through a transparent and participatory process.
4. A selection committee will invite short-listed candidates for interviews, the video recordings of which will thereafter be made public.
5. Every month on its website, the *Lokayukta* will publish a list of cases dealt with, brief details of each, their outcome and any action taken or proposed. It will also publish lists of all cases received by the *Lokayukta* during the previous month, cases dealt with and those which are pending.
6. Investigations of each case must be completed in one year. Any resulting trials should be concluded in the following year, giving a total maximum process time of two years.
7. Losses to the government by a corrupt individual will be recovered at the time of conviction.
8. Government office-work required by a citizen that is not completed within a prescribed time period will result in *Lokpal* imposing financial penalties on those responsible, which will then be given as compensation to the complainant.
9. Complaints against any officer of *Lokpal* will be investigated and completed within one month and, if found to be substantive, will result in the officer being dismissed within two months.
10. The existing anti-corruption agencies [CVC], departmental vigilance and the anti-corruption branch of the [CBI] will be merged into *Lokpal* which will have complete power authority to independently investigate and prosecute any officer, judge or politician.
11. Whistle-blowers who alert the agency to potential corruption cases will also be provided with protection by it.

Difference between Government's and Activists' Drafts of Jan Lokpal Bill

Highlights

Difference between Jan Lokpal Bill and Draft Bill, 2010

Jan Lokpal Bill (Citizen's Ombudsman Bill)	Draft Lokpal Bill (2010)
Lokpal will have powers to initiate *suo moto* action or receive complaints of corruption from the general public.	*Lokpal* will have no power to initiate suo moto action or receive complaints of corruption from the general public. It can only probe complaints forwarded by the Speaker of the *Lok Sabha* or the Chairman of the *Rajya Sabha*.
Lokpal will have the power to initiate prosecution of anyone found guilty.	*Lokpal* will only be an Advisory Body with a role limited to forwarding reports to a "Competent Authority".
Lokpal will have police powers as well as the ability to register FIRs.	*Lokpal* will have no police powers and no ability to register an FIR or proceed with criminal investigations.
Lokpal and the anti-corruption wing of the CBI will be one independent body.	The CBI and *Lokpal* will be unconnected.
Punishments will be a minimum of 1 year and a maximum of up to life imprisonment.	Punishment for corruption will be a minimum of 6 months and a maximum of up to 7 years.

Governments Approach about Whistleblower Protection & Citizen-charter

In a bid to narrow differences on the anti-graft legislation and provide itself some political cover against the threat of a public protest, the Government introduced Citizen's Charter and Grievance Redressal Bill 2011 or *Citizen-charter Bill in Dec 20, 2011* along with the already introduced Whistleblower Protection Law or *Public Interest Disclosure (Protection of Information) Bill, 2010* back in August 2011. Responding to this move, Team Anna issued a statement that: "The government proposes to remove CBI, judiciary, citizen charter, whistle blower protection, Group C and Group D employees from the Lokpal jurisdiction. Wouldn't that reduce Lokpal to an empty tin box with no powers and functions?" This issue remains open between Team Anna & Government.

Campaign for the Jan Lokpal Bill

The first version of the Lokpal Bill drafted by the Government of India headed by United Progressive Alliance in 2010 was considered ineffective by anti-corruption activists from the civil society. These activists, under the banner of India Against Corruption, came together to draft a citizen's version of the Lokpal Bill later called the Jan Lokpal. Public awareness drives and protest marches were carried out to campaign for the bill. However, public support for the Jan Lokpal Bill draft started gathering steam after Anna Hazare, a noted Gandhian announced that he would hold an indefinite fast from 5 April 2011 for the passing of the Lokpal/Jan Lokpal bill. The government has however accepted it. To dissuade Hazare from going on an indefinite hunger strike, the Office of the Prime Minister directed the personnel and law ministries to see how the views of social activists can be included in the bill. On 5 April, the National Advisory Council rejected the Lokpal bill drafted by the government. Union Human Resource Development Minister Kapil Sibbal then met social activists Swami Ganesh and Arvind Kejriwal on 7 April to find ways to bridge differences over the bill. However, no consensus could be reached on 7 April owing to several differences of opinion between the social activists and the Government.

Fast & Agitation—Phase 1

On 7 April 2011, Anna Hazare called for a *Jail Bharo Andolan* (translation: Fill jail movement) from 13 April to protest against the Government's rejection of their demands. Anna Hazare also claimed that his group had received six crore (60 million) text messages of support and that he had further backing from a large number of Internet activists. The outpouring of support was largely free of political overtones; political parties were specifically discouraged from participating in the movement. The fast ended on 9 April, after 98 hours, when the Government accepted most demands due to public pressure. Anna Hazare set a deadline, 15 August, for the passing of the bill in the Parliament, failing which he would start a hunger strike from 16 August. The fast also led to the Government of India agreeing to set up a Joint Drafting Committee, which would complete its work by 30 June 2011.

Fast & Agitation—Phase 2

According to Anna and his team, the Government's version of the Lokpal bill was weak and would facilitate the corrupt to go free apart from several other differences. To protest against this, Anna Hazare announced an "Indefinite Fast" (not to be confused with "Fast until death"). Anna and his team asked for permission from Delhi Police for their fast and agitation at Jantar Mantar or JP Park. Delhi Police gave its permission with certain conditions. These conditions were considered by team Anna as restrictive and against the fundamental constitutional rights and they decided to defy the conditions. Delhi Police imposed Sec 144 CrPC. On 16 August, Anna Hazare was taken into preventive custody by Delhi Police. Senior officers of Delhi Police reached Anna Hazare's flat early in the morning and informed him that he could not leave his home. However, Hazare turned down the request following which he was detained. Anna in his recorded address to the nation before his arrest asked his supporters not to stop the agitation and urged the protesters to remain peaceful. Other members of "India Against Corruption", Arvind Kejriwal, Kiran Bedi, Kumar Vishwas and Manish Sisodia were also taken into preventive custody. Kiran Bedi described the situation as resembling a kind of Emergency (referring to the State of Emergency imposed in 1975 by the Indira Gandhi Govt.). The arrest resulted in a huge public outcry and under pressure, the government released him in the evening of 16 August.

However, Anna Hazare refused to come out of jail, starting his indefinite fast from Jail itself. Manish Sisodia explained his situation as, "Anna said that he left home to go to JP Park to conduct his fast and that is exactly where he would go from here (Tihar Jail). He has refused to be released till he is given a written, unconditional permission".

Unwilling to use forces owing to the sensitive nature of the case, the jail authorities had no option but to let Anna spend the night inside Tihar. Later on 17 August, Delhi Police permitted Anna Hazare and team to use the Ramlila Maidan for the proposed fast and agitation, withdrawing most of the contentious provisions they had imposed earlier. The indefinite fast and agitation began in Ramlila Maidan, New Delhi, and went on for around 288 hours (12 days from 16 August 2011 to 28 August 2011). Some of the Lokpal drafting committee members became dissatisfied with Hazare's tactics as the hunger strike went on for the 11th day: Santosh Hegde, a member of Hazare team who headed the Karnataka Lokayukta, strongly criticized Hazare for his insistence of *"having his way"*, concluding *"I feel I am not in Team Anna any more by the way things are going. These (telling Parliament what to do) are not democratic things."* Swami Agnivesh, another central figure in the Hazare group also distanced himself.

Logjam of Lokpal and Lokayukta Bill, 2011

On 27 December 2011, Lok Sabha Parliament winter session passed controversial Lokpal Bill under title of Lokpal and Lokayukta Bill, 2011, but without constitutional status. Before passing this bill it was introduced in Lok Sabha with key amendments moved. The 10-hour house debate, number of opposition parties claimed introduced bill is weak and wanted it withdrawn. Key amendments that were discussed but defeated were following:

- Including corporates, media and NGOs receiving donations
- Bringing CBI under the purview of Lokpal

Amendments that the house agreed upon were:

- Keeping the defence forces and coast guard personnel out of the purview of the anti-graft ombudsman
- Increasing the exemption time of former MPs from five to seven years

Team Anna rejected the proposed bill describing it as "anti-people and dangerous" even before the Lok Sabha gave its assent. The key notes Team Anna made about rejection were:

- Government will have all the control over Lokpal as it will have powers to appoint and remove members at its will.
- Only 10 per cent political leaders are covered by this Bill.
- Bill was also covering temples, mosques and churches.
- Bill was offering favour to corruption accused by offering them free lawyer service.
- Bill was also unclear about handling corruption within Lokpal office.
- Only five per cent of employees are in its ambit, as Class C & D officers were not included.

Team Anna was also disappointed over following inherent exclusions within tabled government bill.

- Central Bureau of Investigation (CBI) should be merged with the Lokpal, and the anti-corruption bureaus and the Vigilance Departments of the State governments with the Lokayukta.
- The Lokpal and the Lokayukta should have their own investigative wings with exclusive jurisdiction over cases filed under the Prevention of Corruption Act.

- The Lokpal should have administrative and financial control over the CBI, and the appointment of the CBI Director should be independent of any political control.
- The jurisdiction of the Lokpal and the Lokayukta should cover Class C and D officers directly.

This bill was then presented in Rajya Sabha where it hit logjam again.

Parliamentary Actions on the Proposed Legislation

On 27 August 2011, a special and all exclusive session of Parliament was conducted and a resolution was unanimously passed after deliberations in both the houses of Indian Parliament by sense of the house.

The resolution, in principle, agreed on the following subjects and forwarded the Bill to a related standing committee for structure and finalize a report:

- A citizen charter on the bill
- An appropriate mechanism to subject lower bureaucracy to Lokpal
- The establishment of Lokayukta (ombudsmen at state level) in states

On being informed of this development, Anna Hazare, civil rights activists along with protestors at the site of the fast welcomed this development, terming it as a battle "half won" while ending the protest.

THE LOKPAL BILL, 2011

The Lokpal Bill, 2011, also referred to as The Lokpal and Lokayukta Bill, 2011, is a proposed anti-corruption law in India which "seeks to provide for the establishment of the institution of Lokpal to inquire into allegations of corruption against certain public functionaries and for matters connecting them". The bill was tabled in the Lok Sabha on 22 December 2011 and was passed by the house on 27 December 2011 as The Lokpal and Lokayukta Bill, 2011. The bill was subsequently tabled in the Rajya Sabha on 29 December 2011. After a marathon debate that stretched until midnight of the following day, the vote failed to take place for lack of time. On 21 May 2012, the bill was referred to a Select Committee of the Rajya Sabha for consideration. The bill was introduced in parliament following massive public protests led by anti-corruption crusader Anna Hazare and his associates. The bill is one of the most widely discussed and debated bills in India, both by the media and the People of India at large, in recent times. The protests were named among the "Top 10 News Stories of 2011" by the magazine *Time*. The bill received worldwide media coverage. Corruption is an emotional issue in India, where at least 12 whistle-blowers were killed and 40 assaulted after seeking information under a new Right to Information Act aimed at exposing local graft, according to data compiled by Bloomberg L.P. from January 2010 through mid-October 2011. Enacted by Singh six years ago, the legislation became the most powerful tool for fighting wrongdoing in politics and business, with 529,000 requests filed in the year through March. In 2011, India ranked 95th in the Corruption Perceptions Index of Transparency International. A recent survey estimated that corruption in India had cost billions of dollars and threatened to derail growth. India lost a staggering $462 billion in illicit financial flows due to tax evasion, crime and corruption post-Independence, according to a report released by Washington-based Global Financial Integrity.

Union Cabinet Approved Bill

The government moved its version of the bill in the Lok Sabha on 4 August, the ninth such introduction. The bill was introduced by the Minister of State in the Prime Minister's Office, V. Narayanasamy. Leader of Opposition Sushma Swaraj opposed the exclusion of the prime minister from the purview of the proposed Lokpal. V. Narayanasamy told the House that Prime Minister Manmohan Singh was in favour of bringing his office under the purview of the Lokpal, but the Cabinet rejected the idea after deliberation. Anna Hazare burnt copies of the bill, to protest the government's lack of sincerity. The bill was referred to the Parliament's Standing Committee on Personnel, Public Grievances and Law and Justice on 8 August. The committee was headed by Congress Rajya Sabha MP Abhishek Manu Singhvi. The committee of 31 members from across parties was given three months to submit its report. On 27 August the Lok Sabha and Rajya Sabha passed a Pranab Mukherjee-proposed resolution conveying the sense of the House on the Lokpal Bill. The House agreed 'in principle' on a Citizen's Charter, placing the lower bureaucracy under the Lokpal and establishing the Lokayukta in the States.

A high point was noticed on 27 August 27, 2011 when the historic debate leading to the 'Sense of the House' in Parliament on the Lokpal Bill was held. The event reinforced the inviolable primacy of the Indian Constitution. It was also an event of relief and reassurance to the vast and silent majority who constitute India's core civil society.

Journey through The Lok Sabha

The Lokpal was tabled in the Lok Sabha on 22 December 2011 and passed by voice voting on the first day of the three day extended session of the Winter session of the Lok Sabha, on 27 December 2011, after a marathon debate that lasted over 10 hours. The Lokpal body was not given the constitutional status as the Constitutional Amendment Bill, which provided for making the Lokpal a constitutional body, was defeated in the house. The Prime Minister described this as "a bit of disappointment" and added:

We have, however, fulfilled our objective of bringing these bills to Parliament as we had promised.

The bill passed by the house was termed as "useless" by Team Anna and held its view that there was no need of giving such a weak Lokpal a constitutional status. The government withdrew its previous version and had introduced a newer version of the bill. RJD leader Lalu Prasad, along with the support from the other parties like SP, AIMMM and LJP, demanded an inclusion of candidates from minorities in the nine member Lokpal Bench. The government gave in to the demands of parties. The principal opposition party, the BJP, objected to it, classifying that such a move was illegal and asked the government to withdraw the bill. BJD, JDU, RJD, SP, TDP and Left said the bill was weak and wanted it to be withdrawn.

The bill passed by the house deleted the provision that gave presiding officers the power to act against ministers and MPs, even before trial, but the exemption time of former MPs was increased from five to seven years. It excluded armed forces and coast guard from the purview of the anti-graft body. The Lokpal would take complaints against the prime minister after the consent of two-thirds of the Lokpal panel. The consent of state governments is mandatory for the notification to set up Lokayukta in the states, but the setting up of them in the states was made mandatory. The appointment panel is loaded in favour of the government. Mr. Mukherjee also said, during the discussion in the house, that the government has agreed that the Leader of the Opposition and the Chief Justice of India will now be asked to select the chief of the CBI with the Prime Minister. The Lokpal Bill was passed under Article 252 of the constitution of India. Opposition parties objected to this saying that bill could be passed only by Article 253 as the law pertains to public services. The bill didn't relinquish administrative control of the CBI to the Lokpal. The BJP, Left, BSP and SP, all wanted the government should loosen its grip over the CBI. The rationale of such parties was that as long as the government decides the CBI's budget, and the postings and transfers of its officers, the agency is vulnerable to governmental influence. The Prime Minister, making it clear the government's stand on the issue of CBI:

We believe that the CBI should function without interference through any Government diktat. But no institution and no individual, howsoever high he may be, should be free from accountability.

The Bharatiya Janata Party (BJP) abstained from voting on the amendment moved by Basudeb Acharia on bringing corporate houses and the act of the Prime Minister signing commercial agreements under the Lokpal. A number of amendments moved by Opposition to bring the media and NGOs receiving donations were also defeated. The Left, Samajwadi Party and BSP staged a walkout during voting of the bill, protesting that their demands were not being met. With a strength of 277 in the Lok Sabha, the UPA managed to obtain only 243 votes. At least 15 Congress members and close to a dozen belonging to UPA allies were not present at the time of voting. The house also secured the passage of the Whistleblowers Bill.

Journey through The Rajya Sabha

Winter Session, 2011

The ombudsman debate was taken up by The Rajya Sabha during the last day of the three day extension of the winter session of Parliament, but the body recessed on 29 December without voting. The bill was debated for over 12 hours ending abruptly at midnight as the House ran out of scheduled time. The House was adjourned sine die by Chairman Hamid Ansari. A verbal duel marred proceedings as some members including UPA ally Trinamool Congress interrupted V. Narayanasamy's defence of the Bill and a lawmaker snatched papers from a minister and flung them across the chamber. A vociferous opposition insisted on a vote while the government maintained it needed time to reconcile the 187 amendments/confusion marked the proceedings. Ansari asked for the national anthem Jana Gana Mana to be played, signalling the end of the proceedings and told the house:

"This is an unprecedented situation…there appears to be a desire to outshout each other. There is a total impasse. The House cannot be conducted in the noise that requires orderly proceedings, I am afraid the Chair has no option…most reluctantly…I am afraid I can't and..."

After a 15-minute adjournment between 11.30 and 11.45 PM, Pawan Kumar Bansal said that the decision on extension of the House was the government's prerogative. Leader of the Opposition Arun Jaitley charged that the government was running away from Parliament and that the House should decide how long it should sit. He added: You are creating an institution where you control the appointment mechanism, where you control the removal mechanism. We will support the appointment of the Lokpal procedures, but we cannot be disloyal to our commitment to create an integrity institution. Sitaram Yechury (CPI-M) said the House had expected the bill on Wednesday, but it came only on Thursday, the last day of the session. Derek O'Brien, a Trinamool upper house lawmaker, stated that his party could not back the bill because it infringed on states' autonomy. He said "This is a shameful day for India's democracy. The government handled this situation very badly. As the Opposition insisted on a vote, Bansal said the government was willing provided that the House passed the Bill voted by the Lok Sabha on Tuesday. This meant that the proposed amendments would have to be set aside. As stalemate and wrangling continued, the Chairman called an end to the proceedings. Chidambaram defended the deferment of Lokpal and Lokayukta Bill, 2011 in Rajya Sabha on December 29 contending that it was the "only prudent course" before the government and that it had ensured that the Bill remained alive. He continued to attack the BJP and called the amendments an "ingenious" method to scuttle the bill Hazare called off his hunger strike prematurely, blaming poor health.

Budget Session, 2012

Activists pushing hoped that the House would approve the bill towards the end of the second half of the budget session of 2012. The bill was re-introduced in the Rajya Sabha on 21 May 2012. While moving the bill, the minister said that the differences had been narrowed. He said that the government proposed to bring the lower bureaucracy under the Lokpal, which would have investigation and prosecution powers. CVC would monitor Lokpal-referred investigations by the CBI. There would be provisions for attaching properties and a time-frame for investigations. The government proposed that the Bill would be amended to give states the right to pass the bill in their own assemblies. So the national law would not be forced upon states. After the amended bill was introduced, Narayanasamy, Samajwadi Party member Naresh Agrawal sought to send the bill to a *select committee*. This was strongly objected to by BJP, the Left parties and BSP, with their members arguing that only the minister concerned (Narayanasamy) could do so and accusing the ruling coalition of "using the shoulder" of a "friendly opposition" party. After high drama the government yielded and Narayanasamy moved the motion, which immediately passed by voice vote.

The committee met on 25 June and decided on "wider consultations" with the government officials and the public. The panel invited public comments and called representatives of various ministries for recording evidence. The meeting was headed by senior Congress MP Satyavrat Chaturvedi. Law Secretary B. A. Agarwal was summoned to clarify various matters. The committee met again on 19 July 2012. The director of the CBI aired his views in the meeting. He made it clear that the CBI is open to changes in the Lokpal bill that strengthen the agency's autonomy by enhancing the proposed Lokpal's role in key appointments like those of director, head of prosecution and lawyers who represent CBI. He also mentioned in the meeting that the Lokpal should be given a significant say in appointing the director of the prosecution wing instead of the process being controlled by the law ministry as is currently the procedure, the persistent criticism about CBI's investigations being throttled by political directives could be addressed as well. He opposed making the prosecution or the anti-corruption wings subservient to the Lokpal. The select committee had in its earlier sittings examined senior law officials who agreed with the members that the prescription for Lokayukta under Article 253 that refers to fulfilment of international obligations— in this case the UN convention against corruption - might not be feasible. Recourse to international treaties to frame a law that impact the federal structure is not within the ambit of the law. The Select committee referred the Bill for Public Suggestions in July 2012. In reply hundreds of responses were received to the Rajya Sabha. The committee took a view and shortlisted certain recommendations and took Oral Evidence in physical presence of the Members. Committee considered some of the most valid suggestions being done by the Members. Mr. Deepak Tongli of Hyderabad had come with a proposal of setting up the lower most unit to keep regular check on Anti-Corruption in petty cases at District Level. In addition few other members also shared their views in this regard. Mr. Tongli, 26 yrs. aged happened to be the youngest person to appear before the Parliamentary committee for Oral Evidence at Rajya Sabha.

Monsoon Session, 2012

The monsoon session of parliament was to be held in August 2012. Hence, a bill that is pending before the upper house whether or not it was passed by the Lok Sabha, does not lapse on its dissolution. Hence, the bill is still alive in its present form. The bill was not expected to be tabled in the Rajya Sabha before the first day of the last week of the session.

LOKAYUKTA

The Lokayukta (also Lok Ayukta) is an anti-corruption ombudsman organization in the Indian states. The Administrative Reforms Commission (ARC) headed by Morarji Desai submitted a special interim report on "Problems of Redressal of Citizen's Grievances' in 1966. In this report, the ARC recommended the setting up of two special authorities designated as 'Lokpal' and 'Lokayukta' for the redressal of citizens' grievances. The Lokayukta, along with the Income Tax Department and the Anti-Corruption Bureau, mainly helps people bring corruption amongst the politicians and officers in the government service to public attention. Many acts of the Lokayukta have not resulted in criminal or other consequences for those charged. Maharashtra was the first state to introduce the institution of Lokayukta through *The Maharashtra Lokayukta and Upa-Lokayuktas Act in 1971*. This was followed by similar acts being enacted by states of Rajasthan, Bihar, Uttar Pradesh, Karnataka, Madhya Pradesh, Andhra Pradesh, Gujarat and Delhi. Maharashtra Lokayukta is considered as weak due to lack of powers, adequate staff, funds and no independent investigating agency. Karnataka Lokayukta is considered as the most powerful Lokayukta in the country.

Constitutional Amendment for Effectiveness

An amendment to the Constitution has been proposed to implement the Lokayukta uniformly across Indian States. The proposed changes will make the institution of Lokayukta uniform across the country as a three-member body, headed by a retired Supreme Court judge or high court chief justice and comprising the state vigilance commissioner and a jurist or an eminent administrator as other members.

Lokayukta/Lokpal/Lokaayog Acts in Indian States

- Lokayukta, Andhra Pradesh
- Lokayukta, Assam
- Lokayukta, Bihar
- Lok Aayog Adhyadesh (ordinance), Chhattisgarh
- Lokayukta, Delhi
- Lokayukt, Goa
- Lokayukta, Gujarat
- Lokayukta, Haryana
- Lokayukta, Himachal Pradesh
- Lokayukta, Jharkhand
- Lokayukta, Karnataka
- Lokayukta, Kerala
- Lokayukta, Madhya Pradesh
- Lokayukta, Maharashtra
- Lokpal, Orissa
- Lokpal, Punjab
- Lokayukta, Rajasthan
- Lokayukta, Uttarakhand—adopted from Uttar Pradesh
- Lokayukta, Uttar Pradesh

There are no Lokayukta in Arunachal Pradesh, Jammu and Kashmir, Manipur, Meghalaya, Mizoram, Nagaland, Sikkim, Tamil Nadu, Tripura and West Bengal. The latest Lokayukta was established in Goa.

Reforms

In November 2012, after conclusion of the 11th *All India Lokayukta Conference*, as many as 16 Lokayukta sent many recommendations to the Government of India. The recommendations were as follows:

- Make Lokayukta the nodal agency for receiving all corruption complaints.
- Accord Lokayukta jurisdiction over State-level probe agencies.
- Bring bureaucrats under the ambit of the Lokayukta.
- Accord powers of search and seizure and powers to initiate contempt proceedings.
- Provide Lokayukta administrative and financial autonomy.
- Bring Non-Governmental Organizations (NGO) funded by the government under Lokayukta's jurisdiction.

FOCUS ON NATIONAL COMMISSION TO REVIEW THE WORKING OF THE CONSTITUTION

Probity in governance is an essential and vital requirement for an efficient and effective system of governance and for socio-economic development. An important requisite for ensuring probity in governance is absence of corruption. The other requirements are effective laws, rules and regulations governing every aspect of public life and, more important, an effective and fair implementation of those laws, etc. Indeed, a proper, fair and effective enforcement of law is a facet of discipline. Unfortunately for India, discipline is disappearing fast from public life and without discipline, as the Scandinavian economist- sociologist, Gunnyar Myrdal, has pointed out, no real progress is possible. Discipline implies *inter alia* public and private morality and a sense of honesty. While in the West a man who rises to positions of higher authority develops greater respect for laws, the opposite is true in our country. Here, the mark of a person holding high position is the ease with which he can ignore the laws and regulations. We are being swamped by a culture of indiscipline and untruth; morality, both public and private, is at a premium. This paper explores whether some legislative measures can be designed to ensure probity in governance. It is true that instilling a sense of discipline among the citizens is more the function of the society, its leaders, political parties and public figures and less a matter which can be legislated upon. Even so, things have come to such a pass that measures need to be contemplated.

Menace of Corruption in Public Life

Corruption is an abuse of public resources or position in public life for private gain. The scope for corruption increases when control on the public administrators is fragile and the division of power between political, executive and bureaucracy is ambiguous. Political corruption which is sometimes inseparable from bureaucratic corruption tends to be more widespread in authoritarian regimes where the public opinion and the Press are unable to denounce corruption. The paradox of India, however, is that in spite of a vigilant press and public opinion, the level of corruption is exceptionally high. This may be attributed to the utter insensitivity, lack of shame and the absence of any sense of public morality among the bribe-takers. Indeed, they wear their badge of corruption and shamelessness with equal élan and brazenness. The increase of opportunities in State intervention in economic and social life has vastly increased the opportunity for political and bureaucratic corruption, more particularly since politics has also become professionalized. We have professional politicians who are politicians on a full time basis, even when out of office. India is rated at 73 out of 99 countries in the corruption perception index prepared by a non-governmental organization, Transparency International. Corruption today poses a danger not only to the quality of governance but is threatening the very foundations of our society and the State. Corruption in defence purchases, in other purchases and contracts tend to undermine the very security of the State. Some of the power contracts are casting such financial burden upon some of the States that the very financial viability of those States has fallen into doubt. There seems to be a nexus between terrorism, drugs, smuggling, and politicians, a fact which was emphasized in the Vohra Committee Report.

Corruption has flourished because one does not see adequately successful examples of effectively prosecuted cases of corruption. Cases, poorly founded upon, half-hearted and incomplete investigation, followed by a tardy and delayed trial confluence a morally ill-deserved but a legally inevitable acquittal. The acceptance of corruption as an inexorable reality has led to silent reconciliation and resignation to such wrongs. There needs to be a vital stimulation in the social consciousness of our citizens—that is neither has a place in the personal nor social. It is true that the present process of withdrawing the State from various sectors in which it should have never entered or in which it is not capable of performing efficiently may reduce the chances of corruption to some extent but even if we migrate to a free market economy, there has to be regulation of economy as distinct from restrictions upon the industrial activity. The requirements of governance would yet call for entering into contracts, purchases and so on.

The Scandinavian economist-sociologist, Gunnyar Myrdal, had described the Indian society as a 'soft society'. He also clarified what the expression 'soft society' means. According to him, a soft society is: (a) one which does not have the political will to enact the laws necessary for its progress and development and/or does not possess the political will to implement the laws, even when made, and (b) where there is no discipline. In fact, he has stressed the second aspect more than the first. According to him, if there is no discipline in the society, no real or meaningful development or progress is possible. It is the lack of discipline in the society—which expression includes the administration and structures of governance at all levels—that is contributing to corruption. Corruption and indiscipline feed upon each other. One way of instilling the discipline among the society may be to reduce the chances of corruption and to deal with it sternly and mercilessly wherever it is found. For this purpose, the inadequacies in the criminal judicial system have to be redressed. Corruption is also anti-poor. Take, for example, the Public Distribution System (PDS) and the welfare schemes for the poor including Scheduled Castes (SCs) and Scheduled Tribes (STs). It is well-known that a substantial portion of grain, sugar and kerosene oil meant for PDS goes into black-market and that hardly 16% of the funds meant for STs and SCs reach them—all the rest is misappropriated by some of the members of the political and official class and unscrupulous dealers and businessmen. The famous economist, Late Mehbub-Ul-Haq succinctly and poignantly set out the ill-effects of corruption in a South Asian country like ours. He said:

"Corruption happens everywhere. It has been at the center of election campaigns in Italy and the United Kingdom, led to the fall of governments in Japan and Indonesia, and resulted in legislative action in Russia and the United States. But, if corruption exists in rich, economically successful countries, why should South Asia be worried about it? The answer is simple: South Asian corruption has four key characteristics that make it far more damaging than corruption in any other parts of the world.

First, corruption in South Asia occurs up stream, not down stream. Corruption at the top distorts fundamental decisions about development priorities, policies, and projects. In industrial countries, these core decisions are taken through transparent competition and on merit, even though petty corruption may occur down stream.

Second, corruption money in South Asia has wings, not wheels. Most of the corrupt gains made in the region are immediately smuggled out to safe havens abroad. Whereas there is some capital flight in other countries as well, a greater proportion goes into investment. In other words, it is more likely that corruption money in the North Asia is used to finance business than to fill foreign accounts.

Third, corruption in South Asia often leads to promotion, not prison. The big fish— unless they belong to the opposition – rarely fry. In contrast, industrialized countries often have a process of accountability where even top leaders are investigated and prosecuted. For instance, former Italian Prime Minister Bettino Craxi was forced to live in exile in Tunisia to escape extradition on corruption charges in Rome. The most frustrating aspect of corruption in South Asia is that the corrupt are often too powerful to go through such an honest process of accountability.

Fourth, corruption in South Asia occurs with 515 million people in poverty, not with per capita incomes above twenty thousand dollars. While corruption in rich rapidly growing countries may be tolerable, though reprehensible, in poverty stricken South Asia, it is political dynamite when the majority of the population cannot, but to massive human deprivation and even more extreme income meet their basic needs while a few make fortunes through corruption. Thus corruption in South Asia does not lead to simply Cabinet portfolio shifts or newspaper headlines inequalities. Combating corruption in the region is not just about punishing corrupt politicians and bureaucrats but about saving human lives. There are two dimensions of corruption. One is the exploitative corruption where the public servant exploits the helpless poor citizen. The other is collusive corruption where the citizen corrupts the public servant by a bribe because he gets financially better benefits. Collusive corruption depends on black money."

It may be recalled that the Supreme Court had given certain directions in the case of Vineet Narain vs. Union of India (AIR 1998 SC 889) for conferring statutory status upon the Central Vigilance Commission and to insulate the Central Bureau of Investigation and the Enforcement Directorate from political control and pressures. In the said decision, the Supreme Court referred with approval the recommendations of Lord Nolan Committee on Standards in Public Life in the United Kingdom. The following principles of public life, of general application, were commended by the court:

Principles of public life: The general principles of conduct which underpin public life need to be restated. We have done this. The seven principles of selflessness, integrity, objectivity, accountability, openness, honesty and leadership are set out (later on).

Codes of conduct: All public bodies should draw up codes of conduct incorporating these principles.

Independent scrutiny: Internal systems for maintaining standards should be supported by independent scrutiny.

Education: More needs to be done to promote and reinforce standards of conduct in public bodies, in particular through guidance and training, including induction training."

The Seven Principles of Public Life stated in the Report by Lord Nolan

Selflessness: Holders of public office should take decisions solely in terms of the public interest. They should not do so in order to gain financial or other material benefits for themselves, their family, or their friends.

Integrity: Holders of public office should not place themselves under any financial or other obligation to outside individuals or organizations that might influence them in the performance of their official duties.

Objectivity: In carrying out public business, including making public appointments, awarding contracts, or recommending individuals for rewards and benefits, holders of public office should make choices on merit.

Accountability: Holders of public office are accountable for their decisions and actions to the public and must submit themselves to whatever scrutiny is appropriate to their office.

Openness: Holders of public office should be as open as possible about all the decisions and actions that they take. They should give reasons for their decisions and restrict information only when the wider public interest clearly demands.

Honesty: Holders of public office have a duty to declare any private interests relating to their public duties and to take steps to resolve any conflicts arising in a way that protects the public interest.

Leadership: Holders of public office should promote and support these principles by leadership and example.

The Supreme Court observed further:

"These principles of public life are of general application in every democracy and one is expected to bear them in mind while scrutinizing the conduct of every holder of a public office. It is trite that the holders of public offices are entrusted with certain powers to be exercised in public interest alone and, therefore, the office is held by them in trust for the people. Any deviation from the path of rectitude by any of them amounts to a breach of trust and must be severely dealt with instead of being pushed under the carpet. If the conduct amounts to an offence, it must be promptly investigated and the offender against whom a prima facie case is made out should be prosecuted expeditiously so that the majesty of law is upheld and the rule of law vindicated. It is the duty of the judiciary to enforce the rule of law and, therefore, to guard against erosion of the rule of law."

An instance and consequence of the adverse effects of corruption on Indian economy can be gauged from the following statement by Prem Shankar Jha, a keen observer of Indian economy:

"So far, despite adopting some of the most liberal foreign investment laws in Asia, India has not succeeded in seducing even one major international corporation into using it as a global production platform. All the Foreign Direct Investment that has come has been bent upon exploiting the domestic market for consumer goods and durables. In a frank discussion in Singapore, fund managers and corporate executives revealed that the main reason why they were not prepared to mesh India into their global production plans was that even after they had obtained all the clearances from the Central and State Governments, they remained at the mercy of local bureaucrats and politicians. Any one of them could stop their operations, and threatened to do so if they were not given an adequate 'inducement'. Every change of government in a state led to a fresh set of demands and a fresh set of negotiations with the new incumbents. To sum it up, the Chinese took larger bribes, but delivered security of investment in return. Petty bureaucrats who transgressed this principle received a bullet in the back of the head in a football stadium. In India, by contrast, they prospered while the enterprise sickened or died.".

Certain measures required to be taken for ensuring probity in governance. For ensuring probity in governance, several measures are necessary, some of which are mentioned herein below:

A. Need for enforcing section 5 of the Benami Transactions (Prohibition) Act, 1988

While many provisions of the Benami Transactions (Prohibition) Act, 1988 are salutary, it is necessary to take note of some of the anachronisms in the said Act. The expression "benami transaction" is defined in clause (a) of section 2 of the said Act. The said clause reads as under:

'(a) "benami transaction" means any transaction in which property is transferred to one person for a consideration paid or provided by another person;'.

This definition appears to be susceptible to unchartered application taking in *bona fide* transactions which do not injure public interest—say, a father buying a flat for his child, paying the price in instalments. If the money for purchase is accounted for and it is a transaction of advancement, it should not be voided. This is the true meaning and purport of the definition. The Act, a statute containing nine sections, perhaps requires to be modified and strengthened. Section 3 prohibits a person from entering into any benami transaction. Be that as it may, the Act prohibits "benami transactions" and disables any person from claiming that though the property stands in another's name, he himself is the real owner. This Act, enacted as far back as 1988 by Parliament, contains a very salutary and much desired provision in section 5 which reads thus:

Property held benami liable to acquisition: (1) All properties held benami shall be subjected to acquisition by such authority, in such manner and after following such procedures, as may be prescribed.

For the removal of doubts, it is hereby declared that no amount shall be payable for the acquisition of any property under sub-section (1).

It is evident from a reading of section 5 that it can become effective and operational only when rules are made under section 8 prescribing the authority, the manner and procedure following which benami properties can be acquired by the State (without paying any compensation). In fact, section 8 expressly contemplates rules being made by the Central Government for carrying out the purposes of the Act. It is surprising that the Central Government has not so far thought it fit to make rules for the above purpose. The Act is of general application; it applies to every benami transaction, whether the persons concerned are public servants or not. It is imperative that this is done forthwith, thus fulfilling the legislative mandate.

Perhaps, it may be safer to have a separate and exhaustive law relating to public servants. A law in relation to "public servants" as defined by section 2(c) of the Prevention of Corruption Act, 1988 and section 21 of the Indian Penal Code is a prime necessity. Such an Act must be comprehensive in nature and must also deal with acquisition of assets of public servants. The law must provide the manner in which properties can be held by the wife, minor children, near relations of a public servant and should stipulate that if circumstances show that they are benamidars of the public servants (which expression should be defined in the same manner as in section 2(c) of the Prevention of Corruption Act, 1988 and section 21 of the Indian Penal Code), the same should warrant a special provision which would declare the effects of holding of such assets. The statute may also provide that if proper statutory procedures of reporting and verification are not followed, the burden of proof may be placed on the holder of the property to show that the same was not acquired by him benami. It is also suggested that amendments to the Transfer of Property Act, 1882 and the Registration Act, 1908 should be made by which acquisition or transfer of property in favour of or by a public servant would only be through registered instruments warranting prior scrutiny or post-transaction scrutiny. (In Delhi, majority of property transactions are done only on the basis of power of attorney and wills; no registered documents are ever executed—which incidentally means a substantial loss of public revenue by way of stamp duty and registration charges). This may be made applicable even in relation to transactions by which even though a final conveyance may not be executed, yet interest in property may be sought to be passed *de facto*. The provisions may cover not only the public servants but all those within the family of the public servant. There must exist a clear definition of the family of the public servants. The Companies Act, 1961, which has enabled the near and dear ones of the corrupt to float fabulously rich companies through complex cyclical money in poring also needs to be amended. The status—financial and property matters—of a public servant needs to be brought under the proposed comprehensive law relating to public servants. We suggest that in the law, there should be a monitoring mechanism not composed of officials of the executive government (since the executive government can misuse such provisions to retaliate against unwilling civil servants) but an independent Ombudsman who will regulate the civil service. It is needless to add that in addition to stringent provisions relating to public servants, public opinion should encourage concurrent inward digestion of the principles.

It may be recalled that the Benami Transactions (Prohibition) Act, 1988 was made by Parliament about thirteen years ago. It conferred the rule-making power upon the Central Government for the purpose *inter alia* to make rules prescribing the requisite matter contemplated by section 5. The Government has singularly failed in discharging the duty placed upon it by Parliament. It is true that Parliament has not prescribed any time limit for the purpose, but this is no answer. It is never done. In any event, the Central Government must have made the rules within a reasonable time. A period of thirteen years is too long. Central Government cannot frustrate the intent and object of the Parliament by its inaction. Indeed, it is under a statutory obligation to take measures to effectuate the said provision, if the same has not yet been done.

We must also clarify that the principle of the decision of the Supreme Court in A. K. Roy has no application here. Firstly, that was a case of 'conditional legislation' (power to bring a constitutional provision/enactment into force). Secondly, the matter related to the constitutional amendment (to Article 22) effected in 1979 and the case before the Supreme Court came up in 1981 i.e., within about two years. But when the very same question came up before the Supreme Court in 1994 in A.G. of India vs. Amratlal Prajivandas, the nine-Judge Constitution Bench made certain pertinent observations. While observing that it was not necessary to decide the said question for the purpose of that case, the Court noted with approval the argument of the Counsel that such delay on the part of Central Government was not reasonable and that the Parliament while enacting the said amendment Act could never have contemplated that it would be converted into a dead letter by the Central Government by its inaction—deliberate or otherwise.

We are, therefore, of the opinion that at least now the Central Government should enact a comprehensive law on public servants. Such a measure would act as a salutary check—a deterrent—upon corrupt public servants and would certainly be a measure to ensure probity in governance.

In this connection, it is necessary to point out the inadequacies in the existing law, namely, the Prevention of Corruption Act, 1988 and the Indian Penal Code. Mere prosecution under the IPC or the Prevention of Corruption Act (PCA) is not sufficient, apart from the fact that such prosecutions are very rarely launched and even when they are, the conviction is much too rare. Unless the fruits of corruption are taken away, you would not be fighting the corruption truly and effectively. A law for forfeiture of property of corrupt public servants otherwise then through the route of conviction is absolutely essential. In other words, wherever a public servant is found to have screened the illegally acquired assets in the name of a benamidar, action should be taken under this Act and the Rules framed thereunder, and those assets acquired by State without any compensation, as indeed provided for expressly by the Act. For this purpose, the appropriate authority (like the one specified under section 5 of PCA) should be clothed with the necessary powers of investigation, verification, enquiry and the power to gather and receive information from any source, authority, institution or organization. So far as the public servants are concerned, different authorities may be specified in the States and at the Centre. So far as Union and State Ministers are concerned, appropriate authorities have to be created. For non-public servants, appropriate authorities may also have to be specified. The only obligation of such authorities should be to observe the principles of natural justice. It would not be a case of conviction by criminal courts—it would be a purely civil remedy—against corruption. The burden of proving that the property is not held 'benami' should be placed upon the holder of such property/asset.

B. Misfeasance in Public Office—A Remedy

The Supreme Court in an innovative exercise, examined executive actions of two former Union Ministers. It found that one of them allotted petrol pumps in favour of fifteen persons which were plainly vitiated by lack of transparency, nepotism and arbitrariness. The allotments made mostly in favour of the relations of the Ministers or members of his staff. In the case of the other Minister, the Court found that illegal allotments had been made in relation to occupation of Government accommodation. The Court, while taking the view that no public servant could arrogate himself the power to act in a manner which was plainly arbitrary, observed:

"It is high time that the public servants should be held personally responsible for their mala fide acts in the discharge of their functions as public servants. With the change in socio-economic outlook, the public servants are being entrusted with more and more discretionary powers even in the field of distribution of government wealth in various forms. We take it to be perfectly clear, that if a public servant abuses his office either by an act of omission or commission, and the consequence of that is injury to an individual or loss of public property, an action may be maintained against such public servant. No public servant can say "you may set aside an order on the ground of mala fide but you cannot hold me personally liable". No public servant can arrogate to himself the power to act in a manner which is arbitrary." On the question of allotments, the Court opined how the Minister who was executive head of the department held a position of trust. The court observed:

"The government today—in a welfare State—provides large number of benefits to the citizens. It distributes wealth in the form of allotment of plots, houses, petrol pumps, gas agencies, mineral leases, contracts, quotas and licences, etc. Government distributes largesse in various forms. A Minister who is the executive head of the department concerned distributes these benefits and largesse. He is elected by the people and is elevated to a position where he holds a trust on behalf of the people. He has to deal with the people's property in a fair and just manner. He cannot commit breach of trust reposed in him by the people. A transparent and objective criteria/procedure has to be evolved....".

The Supreme Court directed one Minister to pay a sum of ₹ Fifty lakhs by way of exemplary damages to the government. Likewise, the other Minister was asked to pay a sum of ₹ Sixty lakhs by way of exemplary damages. The Court, in both the cases, concluded that the actions of the Ministers amounted to a misfeasance of public property.

The Supreme Court relied upon the well stated position in Ramana Deyaram Shettey and Lucknow Development Authority to hold that in the matter of grant of largesse, the Government and its officials were expected to act in a fair, just and transparent manner and that if they acted in a malicious and deliberate manner causing injury to the citizens of the State, they could be held liable for damages. Rookes v. Barnard was relied upon to hold that exemplary damages could be awarded for "oppressive, arbitrary and unconstitutional action by the servants of the government.". The Supreme Court then concluded:

"We are of the view that the legal position that exemplary damages can be awarded in a case where the action of a public servant is oppressive, arbitrary or unconstitutional is unexceptionable". The same principle was reiterated in the decision concerning the other Minister. It would not be out of place to mention that the Supreme Court followed several other English decisions besides Rookes v. Barnard in arriving at its decision. Indeed the Court pointed out that the principle of Rookes v. Barnard was expressly affirmed by the House of Lords in Broome v. Cassell (1972 AC 1027). The Court also referred to the decision of the Court of Appeals in A. B. v. South West Water Services Ltd. (1993 (1) All E. R. 609) as following and affirming the rule in Rookes v. Barnard. It may also be mentioned that as late as 1996, the U.K. High Court has held in Three Rivers District Council v. Bank of England (1996 (3) All E. R. 558), following earlier decisions that:

"The tort of misfeasance in public office was concerned with a deliberate and dishonest wrongful abuse of the powers given to a public officer and the purpose of the tort was to provide compensation for those who suffered loss as a result of improper abuse of power. It was not to be equated with torts based on an intention to injure, although it had some similarities to them. The tort could be established in two alternative ways: (a) where a public officer performed or omitted to perform an act with the object of injuring the plaintiff (i.e. where there was targeted malice); and (b) where he performed an act which he knew he had no power to perform and which he knew would injure the plaintiff. Accordingly, malice, in the sense of an intention to injure the plaintiff or a person in a class of which the plaintiff was a member, and knowledge by the officer both that he had no power to do the act complained of and that the act or omission would probably (but not that it would necessarily or inevitably) injure the plaintiff or such a person, were alternative, not cumulative, ingredients of the tort. To act with such knowledge was to act in a sufficient sense maliciously.".

This statement of law is indeed a faithful reiteration of the law laid down by the Court of Appeals in Bourgoin S.A. v. Ministry of Agriculture (1985 (3) All E. R. 585).

These decisions, certainly, were welcome and enhanced the image of the Supreme Court in the public eye. The decisions established that courts were concerned with public servants and ministers could not escape consequences of their mala fide acts and orders. The decisions, in substance, demonstrated the adage that "howsoever high you may be, the law is above you". The decisions reinforced the rule of law and not that of men and further that public servants must develop a respect for public property and, above all, that public office is a trust and not a charter of corruption, nepotism and personal gain.

However, the principle enunciated in the above decisions were overruled in a subsequent decision of the Supreme Court in a review petition filed by one of the Ministers. A reading of the judgment (reported in AIR 1999 SC 2979) discloses that the review petition was allowed on the following grounds:

The petitioner before the court "Common Cause", a registered society, was not one of the applicants for allotment of petrol outlets and therefore has not suffered any legal injury by the unlawful allotments made by the Minister. If so, "how could then a finding of commission of misfeasance in public office by the petitioner (the Minister) be recorded in proceedings under Article 32 and that too at the instance of "Common Cause" on the basis of a Press report". Maybe, Common Cause was justified in agitating the said question by way of public interest litigation but that effort has already succeeded inasmuch as the 15 illegal allotments were quashed. But the Court was not entitled to go further and hold that the Minister has committed the tort of misfeasance in public office and to award exemplary damages on that basis.

Damages can be awarded for a tortious act to a particular plaintiff who has suffered loss on account of the said tortious action; "mere allotment of petrol outlets would not constitute 'misfeasance' unless other essential elements were present". True, it is that allotment of 15 outlets by the Minister was wholly unjustified and was an instance of wanton misuse of power, yet "it falls short of 'misfeasance in public office' which is a specific tort and the ingredients of that tort are not wholly met in the case". Hence, there was no occasion to award exemplary damages. Exemplary damages can no doubt be awarded against the public servants in certain situations but not in a case like this. The decision of the House of Lords in Rookes v. Bernard as affirmed in Broome v. Cassell cannot be accepted; "if we were to apply the rule in Rookes v. Bernard as upheld in Cassell and Company Limited v. Broome invariably and unhesitatingly and were to award exemplary damages in every case involving government officers or government servants, the result would be appalling". The Court further observed: "The petitioner does not on becoming the Minister.... assume the role of a 'trustee' in the real sense nor does a 'trust' come into existence in respect of the government properties".

Examined from the point of view of criminal breach of trust as defined in section 405 of the Indian Penal Code, the 'power to allot' cannot be treated as 'property' within the meaning of section 405 IPC that is capable of being misutilized and misappropriated. The direction to initiate criminal proceedings against the Minister concerned was violative of the right to life and liberty guaranteed to him by article 21 of the Constitution. In exercise of its powers under Article 32 of the Constitution, it was not permissible for the Supreme Court "to direct the government to pay the exemplary damages to itself". (This was so held obviously on the footing that a Minister of the government is part of the Government and therefore the Government cannot be directed to pay damages to itself.)

While the moral vigour of the decisions rendered in the aforesaid cases needs to be respected. Whether the principle of damages for a tort of misfeasance must necessarily involve an ingredient of injury to an agreed individual needs to be re-examined. The principle on which liability can be placed on public servants must be clear and must also be a fair principle consistent with need to act fearlessly and must not be capable of comprehending *bona fide* actions, though may be concerned, of civil servants. It is necessary that the principle must promote good governance. By way of example, we may refer to the Andhra Pradesh Cooperative Society's Act, 1964. Section 60 thereof provided that when an office bearer who was entrusted with the organization, affairs of management of the society, misappropriated or fraudulently retained any money or was guilty of any breach of trust, his conduct could be inquired into and an order requiring him to repay or restore the money or property by way of compensation would follow. It is necessary to enact as a part of a comprehensive law relating to public servants, the principles on the basis of which misfeasance can be rendered punishable. The principle must ensure that the wrong-doing is palpably evident, and given the barest standards of foreseeability, no two views are possible. It is then, and then alone, that the public servant is exposed to damages. Likewise, the principle may deal with both the situations, i.e., a situation where a definite injury had been caused to a third person and secondly where a declaration of wanton abuse of power can be arrived at by satisfying judicially manageable standards. Public servants in both the cases must be visited with the imposition of damages. Likewise, the principles of quantification of damages need to be defined since arbitrariness in arriving at figures may well become an area (of non-liquet) where 'no human law and justice may ever reach'. While drafting the legal provisions, there must be an examination of the basic power structure, the composition of the elite, of their fundamental structures in [see W. Michael Reisman, Folded Lies: Bribery, Crusades and Reforms, 69–73 (1973)]. It is necessary that the principles must be clear and achieve the desired result since there have been far too many moral crusades but few successful prosecutions. While adjusting the *bona fide*s or mala fides of an executive act, the matter should be one which is determinable contemporaneously with reference to clear standards of foreseeability.

Section 60 of the Andhra Pradesh Cooperative Societies Act, which carries the heading "Surcharge" reads as follows:

"Surcharge.- (1) Where in the course of an audit under section 50 or any inquiry under section 51 or an inspection under section 52 or section 53, or the winding up of a society, it appears that any person who is or was entrusted with the organization, affairs or management of the society or any past or present officer or servant of the society has misappropriated or fraudulently retained any money or other property or has been guilty of breach of trust in relation to the society or has caused any deficiency in the assets of the society by breach of trust or willful negligence or has made any payment contrary to the provisions of this Act, the rules or the bye-laws, the Registrar himself, or any person specially authorized by him in this behalf, of his own motion or on the application of the committee, liquidator or any creditor or contributory, may inquire into the conduct of such person or officer or servant and make an order requiring him to repay or restore the money or property or any part thereof with interest at such rate as the Registrar or the person authorized as aforesaid thinks just or to contribute such sum to the assets of the society by way of compensation in respect of the misappropriation, misapplication of funds, fraudulent retainer, breach of trust or willful negligence as the Registrar or the person authorized as aforesaid thinks just:

Provided that no order shall be passed against any person referred to in this sub-section unless the person concerned has been given an opportunity of making his representation.

(2) This section shall apply notwithstanding that such person or officer or servant may have incurred criminal liability by his act."

It may be remembered that a cooperative society has an elected managing committee to run and manage its affairs/business and also staff appointed to assist the persons in management in their duties. Both elected members and the employees so appointed are within the ambit of the above section. There is no reason why this principle cannot be extended to the governing machinery at the Union and State level, where too elected members form the government and run and manage the affairs of the State with the assistance of a permanent bureaucracy. Even the statutory authorities should be within the purview of this rule. The protective clauses usually found in enactments only save the authorities from any suit or prosecution in respect of acts done by them in 'good faith'. The protection does not and should not extend to acts done mala fide. Where the mala fide action causes loss to the State, i.e. people as such, the State must be entitled to recover the loss from the concerned official/ authority.

Several other enactments concerning the cooperative societies enacted by the various States too contain similar provisions.

A comprehensive law needs to be enacted to provide that where public servants cause loss to the State by their mala fide actions or omissions of a palpable character to be defined, they should be made liable to make good the loss caused by him to the State and, in addition, would be open to the imposition of exemplary damages. The principles must include cases of misuse of official position and acts outside authority. The expression 'public servant' must be extended to 'all public servants as defined in the Indian Penal Code and in the Prevention of Corruption Act, 1988, which expression has been interpreted to include Members of Parliament, Members of State Legislatures and Councils and Ministers. Such a law would have the merit of obviating several questions like whether Government can be asked to pay damages to itself, whether the power to grant or allot some benefit can be called 'property', whether such action of the public servant constitutes a 'tortuous action', whether damages/ exemplary damages can be awarded for such acts, and if so, on what basis and to what extent, whether public office is a trust and questions of 'locus standi' and so on. It would also contribute to avoidance of multiplicity of proceedings and would be more effective than a mere criminal prosecution, whether under IPC or PC Act. The law must, however, provide that proceedings thereunder can be taken on the basis of information received including an audit report or a report of any commission, committee or body competent to examine the relevant facts. The authority empowered to take proceedings must be an independent high level officer/agency whose tenure, conditions of service and independence should be firmly and fully guaranteed as has been done in the case of Central Vigilance Commissioner. Different authorities may be prescribed for different classes of public servants. For example Ministers and Legislators may constitute one category, Group A officers may constitute another category and so on. Classification can also be done department-wise. This is, however, a matter for the

Parliament/Legislature to decide. It may be appropriate for the Parliament and also State Legislatures on similar lines to enact a new comprehensive law to deal with public servants with reference to their public functions, relationship with the State as well as the examination of their personal effects and private properties. The fact, however, remains that such a course has become absolutely essential and urgent.

The public servants must be put on notice that they will be responsible to make good the loss caused by them to the State by their mala fide acts, to use a comprehensive expression to done the grounds mentioned herein above—that they should no longer be under the cozy impression that all that would happen in such a case is that their mala fide order or action would be set aside by the Court but that nothing would happen to them personally. They should be made aware that a mala fide act or action on their part carries the liability for damages/compensation. Creating personal liability of this kind would contribute greatly to good governance and would emphasize the need for transparent, fair and honest exercise of power. It would in no way dampen the initiative of the Ministers or officials nor would it inhibit them in any manner in effective discharge of their functions. A responsible government and the concept of accountability are not antithetical to good governance; on the contrary they promote it—they contribute to public good. Mere errors of judgment or *bona fide* mistakes would certainly not expose the public servants to such a consequence but where their actions are mala fide, i.e., falling within any of the six grounds mentioned hereinabove, they should be held responsible. If such acts result in loss to the State, they must be made liable to make good the same.

C. Necessity for a law providing for confiscation of illegally acquired assets of public servants

In the decision reported in Delhi Development Authority v. Skipper Construction Co. (P) Ltd. (AIR 1996 SC 2005), the Supreme Court made the following observations:

"... a law providing for forfeiture of properties acquired by holders of 'public office' (including the offices/posts in the public sector corporations) by indulging in corrupt and illegal acts and deals, is a crying necessity in the present state of our society. The law must extend not only to—as does SAFEMA—properties acquired in the name of the holders of such property but also to properties held in the names of his spouse, children or other relatives and associates. Once it is proved that the holder of such office has indulged in corrupt acts, all such properties should be attached forthwith. The law should place the burden of proving that the attached properties were not acquired with the aid of monies/properties received in the course of corrupt deals upon the holder of that property as does SAFEMA whose validity has already been upheld by this Court in the aforesaid decision of the larger Constitution Bench. Such a law has become an absolute necessity, if the canker of corruption is not to prove the death-knell of this nation. According to several perceptive observers, indeed, it has already reached near-fatal dimensions. It is for the Parliament to act in this matter, if they really mean business."

Indeed, in the above case the Supreme Court followed the law laid down by a nine-judge Constitution Bench in Attorney General of India vs. Amratlal Prajivandas [1994

(5) SCC 54] while dealing with the constitutional validity of the Smugglers and Foreign Exchange Manipulators (Forfeiture of Property) Act, 1976 (13 of 1976) which provided a similar forfeiture of illegally acquired assets of smugglers and foreign exchange violators. The nine-judge Bench, in a unanimous decision observed that the laudable object behind the said enactment was:

"to forfeit the illegally acquired properties of the convict/detenue irrespective of the fact that such properties are held by or kept in the name of or screened in the name of any relative or associate as defined in the said two Explanations. The idea is not to forfeit the independent properties of such relatives or associates which they may have acquired independently but only to reach the properties of the convict/detenue or properties traceable to him, wherever they are, ignoring all the transactions with respect to those properties.".

SAFEMA, it may be pointed out, placed the burden of proof squarely upon the smuggler and foreign exchange manipulator to establish that the assets owned by him or by the members of his family have been lawfully acquired. It was pointed out in the said nine-judge Bench decision that such a course was inevitable in the light of the fact that only the person who acquired properties can explain how he has come to acquire those properties and that it is not possible for the authority to do so. It was observed in the said decision:

"... The violation of foreign exchange laws and laws relating to export and import necessarily involves violation of tax laws. Indeed, it is well known fact that over the last few decades, smuggling, foreign exchange violation, tax evasion, drugs and crime have all got mixed-up. Evasion of taxes is integral to such activity. It would be difficult for any authority to say, in the absence of any accounts or other relevant material that among the properties acquired by smuggler, which of them or which portions of them are attributable to smuggling and foreign exchange violations and which properties or which portions thereof are attributable to violations of other laws (which the Parliament has the power to make). It is probably for this reason that the burden of proving that the properties specified in the show cause notice are not illegally acquired properties is placed upon the person concerned. May be this is the case where a dangerous disease requires a radical treatment. Bitter medicine is not bad medicine. In law it is not possible to say that definition is arbitrary or is couched in unreasonably wide terms...."

It is, therefore, quite appropriate that even in the proposed legislation to forfeit the properties of corrupt public servants, the burden of proof should be placed upon the holders of the property. This indeed is the principle of section 106 of the Indian Evidence Act, 1872. The said section along with the illustration appended to it reads as follows:

"Burden of proving fact especially within knowledge: When any fact is especially within the knowledge of any person, the burden of proving that fact is upon him.

Illustrations

(a) When a person does an act with some intention other than that which the character and circumstances of the act suggest, the burden of proving that intention is upon him.

(b) A is charged with traveling on a railway without a ticket. The burden of proving that he had a ticket is on him."

It is on this principle that in prevention of corruption statutes, the burden of proof is very often laid upon the accused. It has been held by the Supreme Court in C. S. D. Swami *versus* State (AIR 1960 SC 7) that "... the Legislature has, thus, deliberately cast a burden on the accused not only to offer a plausible explanation as to how he came by his large wealth, but also to satisfy the Court that his explanation was worthy of acceptance". This case was decided with reference to section 5(3) of Prevention of Corruption Act, 1947. The Court observed further "... section 5(3) of the Act does not create a new offence but only lays down a rule of evidence, enabling the Court to raise a presumption of guilt in certain circumstances" – and thus an exception to the general rule of burden of proof in criminal cases. To the same effect is the decision in State of Maharashtra *versus* Wasudeo (1981 SC 1186). Construing section 5, the Court held: "When section 5(1)(e) uses the words "for which the public servant is unable to satisfactorily account", it is implied that the burden is on such public servant to account for the sources for the acquisition of disproportionate assets", and that if he fails to satisfactorily account for his assets, he is liable to be convicted.

It is pointed out by some that where the property has been acquired several years ago, the person called upon to prove the sources of such acquisition may be under a severe handicap, inasmuch as he may not have kept or preserved the records relating to sources of such acquisition. This is however an aspect which the Court or Tribunal would certainly keep in mind while determining whether the person has discharged the burden that lay upon him.

The philosophical basis for such confiscation was explained by the Supreme Court in, the Attorney General of India, by invoking the concept of 'implied trust'. The relationship between the government and the public servant is of a fiduciary nature. In such a case, it was held, any benefit obtained by a fiduciary through a breach of duty belongs in equity to the beneficiary. It was further observed that a gift accepted by a person in a fiduciary position as an incentive for breach of his duty constituted a bribe and although in law it belonged to the fiduciary, in equity he not only became a debtor for the amount of the bribe to the person to whom the duty was owed, but he also held the bribe and any property acquired therewith on 'constructive trust' for that person. Any increase in the value of such property belonged to the person injured/beneficiary and that in case of any diminution in the asset, the wrong-doer was liable in person. It was also observed that unless there is a law providing for prompt forfeiture of illegally acquired assets, they would be spirited away beyond our shores to safe havens and numbered accounts.

Acting upon the observations of the Supreme Court in the above two judgments, the Law Commission of India submitted its 166th Report on "the Corrupt Public Servants (Forfeiture of property) Bill" recommending to the Central Government to introduce a Bill in Parliament for forfeiture of illegally acquired properties of corrupt public servants. A draft Bill was also enclosed to the said Report. It is again a matter of regret that the government has not thought it fit to take the desired steps.

We are of the opinion that a law as recommended hereinabove, has become absolutely inescapable in today's situation. It would clothe the State with an effective means of checking corruption. Nobody suggests that such an enactment would by itself check corruption. But even if a handful of cases concerning some notoriously corrupt persons are dealt with under such enactment, it will have a sobering effect upon other wrong-doers.

D. Enactment of a Public Interest Disclosure Act

One of the measures adopted in several western countries to fight corruption and mal-administration is enactment of Public Interest Disclosure Acts, which are popularly called Whistle-blower Acts. The object of such enactments is to improve accountability in government and public sector organizations by encouraging people not to turn a blind eye to malpractice taking place in their organizations and to report the same to the specified authority. The motto of the British Act (Public Interest Disclosure Act, 1998) is "Address the message rather than the messenger; and resist the temptation to cover up serious malpractices". The Act provides for protection of Whistle-blowers from dismissal and victimization by making appropriate provisions in that behalf.

An experienced corrupt public servant knows how to circumvent internal control proceedings. Such person indulges in such activity either by himself or in collusion with others, whether employees or outsiders. Even so, wherever corruption or malpractice takes place, it cannot but be that some or the other person in the organization knows it or comes to know of it. The Act enables such person to lay such information before the specified authority and thus promote public interest. It is true that such Whistle-blowing has been looked upon until now with some kind of disfavour, but recently a growing recognition has dawned upon all concerned that the persons who sound the alarm of serious malpractice, corruption or fraudulent activity in government or public sector organizations deserve public thanks and support rather than punished and humiliated for being 'disloyal' to their employers or colleagues.

The Act is really aimed at improving accountability within the government and public sector by allowing the employees to inform the appropriate authorities of organizational or individual wrong doing either in a confidential manner or by a public report. The Act should provide that the authority receiving such information should be an independent person and not be a part of the concerned government or public sector organization. If any information is received by him confidentially containing some allegations, he must investigate the same without publicly humiliating the suspect or the Whistle-blower. He must adopt appropriate methods to ensure the same. It must also be ensured that the persons who lay correct and true information about such illegalities should be rewarded which need not necessarily be financial in nature. It is equally necessary to ensure that this Whistle-blowing facility is not abused by malicious employees, out to achieve their personal grievance or vendetta.

Indeed, it is now believed that the law and the society must help create a culture wherein honest interchanges are respected and valued rather than punished. The Act must ensure that the informants are protected against retribution and any form of discrimination for reporting what they perceived to be wrong doing, i.e., for *bona fide* disclosures which may ultimately turn out to be not entirely or substantially true. It must be recognized, at the same time, that there are certain pitfalls in such a measure in the sense that it is liable to be abused by persons out of vindictiveness or for the purpose of retaliation or for claiming rewards. It must, however, be left to the appropriate authority to determine whether information laid before him confidentially is substantially correct information or whether the informant was acting *bona fide* or whether it is a totally false information actuated by malice or vindictiveness. There must be a provision for punishing persons who lay false information out of such inadmissible motives. It is believed in many developed countries that while there are certainly some risks inherent in such a legislative measure, it is better to run these risks rather than allow corruption and fraud to continue or to leave the Whistle-blower to go to an outside agency. Undoubtedly, the balance between asking people to blow the whistle and telling them that they themselves could be subject to proceedings for laying incorrect information, is a fine one. The situations arising under such a legislative measure, if handled sensitively, may certainly prove a step forward rather than a step backward in the fight against corruption and mal-administration.

In the British Act, the person/authority specified to receive complaints of the above nature is called a regulator.

As the London Borough, Lambeth says in its Whistle Blowing Charter, "if you believe something is wrong, speak out".

In this connection, it would not be out of place to refer to an organization in U.K., "Public Concern At Work", active in this field which has received the recognition of the government of the U.K. In their White Paper, 'The Governance of Public Bodies', the government has accepted the important role Whistle-blowing can play in ensuring probity and accountability and in that connection referred to the said organization as 'the leading organization in this field'. The said organization has published a number of papers espousing the cause of Whistle-blowing including some case studies. It is stated in one of their papers as below:

Standards in Public Life

In policy terms the most important development in recent years has been the Nolan Committee's endorsement of whistle-blowing as a means of ensuring and demonstrating high standards in public bodies. Nolan's 1996 recommendations, which are reproduced on the back cover, were accepted by the Major Government in its 1997 White Paper on The Governance of Public Bodies. The work of the Committee has also clarified the meaning of whistle-blowing. As the White Paper remarks, "The Nolan Committee used the term 'whistle-blowing' to mean the confidential raising of problems within an organization or within an independent review structure associated with that organization, not in the popular pejorative sense of leaking information to the media."

We have also looked into the whistle-blower Acts enacted by various countries viz., U.K., Australia, State of Michigan (USA) and Canada. We find that the Australian Act can serve as a model for our country, no doubt, with appropriate changes. In this connection, we may refer to the episode relating to "Pentagon Papers" which ultimately resulted in the decision of the U.S. Supreme Court in New York Times v. United States (1971) 403 U.S. 713 = 29 L. Ed. 2d. 822. One of the employees, Daniel Ellsberg, working in the defence department, came across a classified study entitled "History of the U.S. Decision-making Process on Vietnam Policy". The study disclosed that the U.S. government has been withholding from public true and correct information regarding its involvement in Vietnam and that it has been guilty of misrepresenting to the American people the issues and the facts relating to their involvement in Vietnam conflict and other relevant facts vitally affecting the American lives and interests. He did not know whom to complain. There was no authority outside the government to whom he could turn. He therefore approached the two leading U.S. dailies, The New York Times and The Washington Post with the material (he had secretly made copies of it). The employee was arrested and harassed for allegedly compromising the national security. The government tried unsuccessfully to block the publication of the said study, popularly known as 'Pentagon Papers' in the aforesaid dailies. The affair turned out to be a serious embarrassment to the U.S. government, and to its successive Presidents responsible for the American involvement in Vietnam.

It is obvious that had there been an independent authority ('Regulator') to whom the employee could have turned with the information in his possession and had such authority been empowered to enquire into the matter and make necessary orders—and if called for in public interest, gone public with it, the proceedings would have ended in an orderly manner and public interest served much better and more promptly. It could also have saved many lives, both American and Vietnamese. It goes without saying that these disclosures led to public disenchantment with—nay, opposition to—Vietnam war in U.S. and to its ultimate withdrawal from Vietnam on 30th April, 1975.

It is understood that the Law Commission of India is in the process of drafting a Public Interest Disclosure Bill, for forwarding it to the Government of India.

E. Enactment of a Freedom of Information Act

Right to receive and the right to impart information has been held to be a part of freedom of speech and expression guaranteed by sub-clause (a) of clause (1) of article 19 of the Constitution subject of course to the reasonable restrictions, if any, that may be placed on such right in terms of and to the extent permitted by clause (2) of the said article. It has been held by the Supreme Court in Secretary, Ministry of I&B vs. Cricket Association of Bengal (1995 (2) SCC 161) that:

"The freedom of speech and expression includes right to acquire information and to disseminate it. Freedom of speech and expression is necessary, for self-expression which is an important means of free conscience and self-fulfillment. It enables people to contribute to debates on social and moral issues. It is the best way to find a truest model of anything, since it is only through it that the widest possible range of ideas can circulate. It is the only vehicle of political discourse so essential to democracy. Equally important is the role it plays in facilitating artistic and scholarly endeavours of all sorts. The right to communicate, therefore, includes right to communicate through any media that is available whether print or electronic or audio-visual such as advertisement, movie, article, speech, etc. That is why freedom of speech and expression includes freedom of the press. The freedom of the press in turn includes right to circulate and also to determine the volume of such circulation. This freedom includes the freedom to communicate or circulate one's opinion without interference to as large a population in the country, as well as abroad, as is possible to reach.".

The fundamental values underlying the concept of freedom of speech, and the functions that the freedom serves in a democratic society, are widely accepted. They can be summarized in the following form:

(i) First, freedom of speech is essential to the development of the individual personality. The right to express oneself and to communicate with others is central to the realization of one's character and potentiality as a human being. Conversely, suppression of thought or opinion is an affront to a person's dignity and integrity. In this respect freedom of speech is an end in itself, not simply an instrument to attain other ends. As such it is not necessarily subordinate to other goals of the society.

(ii) Second, freedom of speech is vital to the attainment and advancement of knowledge. As John Stuart Mill pointed out, an enlightened judgment is possible only if one is willing to consider all facts and ideas, from whatever source, and to test one's conclusion against opposing views. Even speech that conveys false information or maligns ideas, has value, for it compels us to retest and rethink accepted positions and thereby promotes greater understanding. From this function of free speech, it follows that the right to express oneself does not depend upon whether society judges the communication to be true or false, good or bad, socially useful or harmful. All points of view, even a minority of one, are entitled to be heard.

(iii) Third, freedom of speech is a necessary part of our system of democratic government. Sovereignty resides in the people; in other words, the people are the masters and the government is their servant. If the people are to perform their role as sovereign and instruct their government, they must have access to all information, ideas, and points of view. This right of free speech is crucial not only in determining policy but in checking the government in its implementation of policy. The implication of this position is that the government has no authority to determine what may be said or heard by the citizens of the community.

(iv) Fourth, freedom of speech is vital to the process of peaceful social change. It allows ideas to be tested in advance before action is taken, it legitimizes the decision reached, and it permits adaptation to new conditions without the use of force. It does not eliminate conflict in a society, but it does direct conflict into more rational, less violent, channels. In the words of Justice William J. Brennan in New York Times v. Sullivan (1964), speech may often be "uninhibited, robust, and wide-open".

It would not be out of place to quote from the oft-quoted judgment of Brandies J. in Whitney v. California, the following observation:

"... that the greatest menace to freedom is an inert people; that public discussion is a political duty; and that this should be a fundamental principle of the ... government.".

It must be recognized at the same time that today the freedom of expression and in particular the freedom of information is under a grave threat. The "free market-place of ideas"—an expression used in several U.S. Supreme Court judgments to denote freedom of speech and expression—is analogous to the more general argument for a "free market economy", as is opined by Milton Friedman and Jane Friedman in their book "Free to Choose". As indeed pointed out by Jerome Barron (Access to Press—A new First Amendment Right—80 Harvard Law Review 1641-1967) "... if ever there were a self-operating market place of ideas, it has long ceased to exist.... There is inequality in the power to communicate ideas just as there is inequality in economic bargaining power; to recognize the latter and deny the former is quixotic.... Changes in the communications industry have destroyed the equilibrium in that market place. While it may have been still possible in 1925 to believe with Justice Holmes that every idea is "acted on unless some other belief outweighs it or some failure of energy stifle the movement at its birth", it is impossible to believe it now. Yet the Holmesian theory is not abandoned, even though the advent of Radio and television has made even more evident that philosophy's unreality...." Another jurist Herbert Marcuse similarly argues that "under the rule of monopolistic media—themselves the mere instruments of economic and political power—a mentality is created from which right and wrong, true and false are pre-defined whenever they affect the vital interests of society" (Repressive Tolerance by Herbert Marcuse). How much more true all this sounds today when the television and other means of mass communication have become all-pervasive and all-encompassing. What they represent passes for information and truth and our ideas and views are imperceptibly formed by what we hear on television or read in newspapers. It is true that Press and media perform an important and essential function in a democratic society and that notwithstanding their ownership being in the hands of business tycoons and notwithstanding their dependence on government-sponsored advertisements, they are performing a highly valuable and useful function as guardian of the citizens' right to know and their right to impart their ideas and views to the government and the public. As has been rightly observed:

"The functions that freedom of the press performs in a democratic society are, in general, the same as those served by the system of freedom of expression as a whole. Freedom of the press enhances the opportunity to achieve individual fulfillment, advances knowledge and the search for understanding, is vital to the process of self-government, and facilitates social change by the peaceful interchange of ideas. More particularly the press has been conceived as playing a special role in informing the public and in monitoring the performance of government. Often referred to as the "fourth estate," or the fourth branch of government, an independent press is one of the principal institutions in our society that possesses the resources and the capacity to confront the government and other centers of established authority. This concept of a free press was forcefully set forth by Justice Hugo L. Black in his opinion in New York Times Co. v United States (1971) (The Pentagon Papers case): "In the first Amendment, the Founding Fathers gave the free press the protection it must have to fulfill its essential role in our democracy. The press was to serve the governed, not the governors. The government's power to censor the press was abolished so that the press would remain forever free to censure the government. The press was protected so that it could bare the secrets of government and inform the people. Only a free and unrestrained press can effectively expose deception in government."

The Press is thus an important agent in ensuring the citizens' right to receive and impart information as a measure of ensuring probity in governance.

Realising the importance of the freedom of speech and expression including the freedom to receive and impart information, some of the advanced countries have enacted Freedom of Information Acts. The object behind these enactments is to ensure that the governmental activity is transparent, fair and open. Except in matters of defence, atomic energy and matters concerning the security of the country, there is no room for secrecy in the affairs of the government. Whether it is a matter of taking a decision affecting the people or whether it is a transaction involving purchase or sale of government property or whether the matter relates to entering into contracts—in all these matters, the government should act in a transparent manner which means that any and every citizen who wishes t o obtain any information with respect to any of those matters should be entitled to receive it. In this connection, we may usefully refer to the Freedom of Information Act, 2000 enacted by the British Parliament on 30 November, 2000. The main purpose of the Act is to implement the principles set out in the White Paper insofar as it is appropriate to do so by primary legislation. Other matters will be dealt with in secondary legislation, codes of practice or by administrative action. The Act provides a right of access to recorded information held by public authorities, creates certain exemptions from the duty to disclose information and establishes arrangements for enforcement and appeal. The Act amends the Data Protection Act, 1998 and the Public Records Act, 1958. Since the Act purports to implement the principles set out in the White Paper which was issued in December 1997, it may be appropriate to briefly refer to them. In the White Paper entitled "Your Right to Know: the Government's Proposals for a Freedom of Information Act", the following scheme of the Act was indicated:

The new Act will provide for any individual, company or other body to have a right of access to records or information of any data held by a wide range of public bodies. Applicants need not state their purpose in applying for information. The authorities are bound to make certain information public as a matter of course. Indeed, the authorities covered by the Act are required to make certain information publicly available without request (these include facts and analyses which the government considers important in framing major policy proposals, explanatory material on dealing with the public, operational information on costs, standards, targets and complaints procedures of public servants) and further give reasons for administrative decisions. There should be no ministerial veto to prevent disclosures.

What is more, there is no exclusion in favour of the Cabinet or Cabinet Committees from the purview of the Act. Access will be allowed to documents and not merely to information. Of course, security and intelligence services are excluded from the purview of the Act.

There is a similar exclusion—which has attracted a lot of criticism—in favour of criminal and civil enforcement proceedings and the investigation and prosecution functions of the police, prosecutors and "other bodies carrying out law enforcement work such as the Department of Social Security or the Immigration Service", as well as the public sector employment records. There are certain other exemptions too. In view of the above scheme of the English Act, it may not be necessary to refer to its provisions at any length. The Government of India too has recognized the importance of this right and has accordingly introduced a Bill called the Freedom of Information Bill, 2000 (Bill No. 98 of 2000) in Lok Sabha on 25 July 2000. The Bill, as it stands, does ensure to a large extent the freedom of information to citizens with respect to the functioning of the government. It casts an obligation upon public authorities to furnish such information wherever asked for. It would have been better if the said Bill had also provided for the government making information public, without a request therefor from anyone, concerning matters involving major policy proposals and the major multilateral agreements proposed to be entered into. This is for the reason that very often the people who are really going to be affected by such policies and agreements are not even aware of them. The experience of WTO Agreements signed by the Government of India in 1994, without taking the Parliament or the States or the people into confidence, and without a national debate on the pros and cons of the said Agreements, is a telling example. Purporting to exercise their power under article 73 read with article 253 and entry 14 of List I of the Seventh Schedule to the Constitution, the Union Government has concluded several agreements covering not only the subjects in Lists I and III of the said Schedule but also with respect to subjects in List II, which are in the exclusive domain of the States—for example, Agriculture and Public Health. The negative effects of the said Agreements are becoming evident with each passing day and are seriously eroding the viability of the domestic industries (which were built up with huge public funds), agriculture and trade. Be that as it may, the said Bill fills a great void though, it is true, several improvements are possible in it. It is understood that the said Bill has been referred to a Standing Committee. We are enclosing herewith a copy of the recently enacted South African Freedom of Information Act (the promotion of Access to Information Act, 2000) (Annexure) which covers both the public bodies and private bodies. It can indeed serve as a model enactment for any country committed to concept of freedom of information. The necessity and importance of an early enactment in terms of the said Bill—with some improvements—cannot be over-emphasized. It would be useful to notice the various provisions of the English Act and the South African Act before finalizing the draft of the proposed Indian legislation.

F. Necessity for enacting a Lok Pal Bill in addition to the Central Vigilance Commission Act

Institution of Lok Pal

Another measure for ensuring probity in governance is the enactment of a Lok Pal Act and a Central Vigilance Commission Act. It would be appropriate to deal with the Lok Pal Act first. In their interim report on the "Problem of Redress of Citizens' Grievances" submitted in 1966, the Administrative Reforms Commission recommended *inter alia* the setting up of the institution of Lok Pal. To give effect to this recommendation, a Bill called the Lok Pal and Lokayukta Bill, 1968 was introduced in the fourth Lok Sabha in 1968. It was referred to a Joint Committee of the two Houses of Parliament and on the basis of its Report, the Bill was passed by Lok Sabha in 1969. But while the Bill was pending in the Rajya Sabha, the fourth Lok Sabha was dissolved with the result that the Bill lapsed.

In 1971, the Bill passed by the previous Lok Sabha was reintroduced in Lok Sabha under the same title but this Bill also lapsed on the dissolution of the fifth Lok Sabha. The Bills introduced in 1968 and 1971 covered complaints in respect of not only allegations of misconduct but also grievances as to mal-administration. Lok Pal was thought of as a single member body who could be described roughly as a person who would combine in himself the functions of ombudsman as known to the western countries such as Norway, Sweden, UK and the functions of the Central Vigilance Commission as it was constituted under an administrative order of the Central Government. Complaints could be made under the said Bill against the union ministers, union civil servants, union territory ministers and persons in the service of local authorities and corporations, owned or controlled by the Central Government. However, Members of Parliament and the State Chief Ministers were not covered by the Bill. In short, these Bills were designed to check abuse of power, corruption and other instances of mal-administration; liberty was given to the aggrieved persons to approach specified authorities.

In the year 1977, a fresh Bill called the Lok Pal Bill, 1977 was introduced in Lok Sabha. It was again referred to a Joint Committee of both Houses of Parliament which submitted its Report in July 1978. While this Bill was under consideration of the Lok Sabha, it was prorogued first and subsequently dissolved. Accordingly, this Bill also lapsed. It may be mentioned that the 1977 Bill did not take in grievances as to mal-administration; it was confined to complaints as to misconduct or corruption against specified categories of persons including Union Ministers, Members of Parliament, State Chief Ministers and so on. This Bill brought within its purview the Prime Minister and MLAs of Union Territories as well. Civil servants were excluded from its purview. The definition of 'misconduct' was widely worded to include instances of abuse of power wherein a public man—if we can use that expression to denote the persons brought within the purview of the Act—directly or indirectly, allows his position to be taken advantage of by his relatives or associates. The Bill also provided that a public man would be guilty of misconduct if he fails to act in accordance with norms of integrity and conduct which ought to be followed by the class of public men to which he belongs. Of course, the Joint Committee to which this Bill was referred had recommended that the said requirement be omitted. Be that as it may, this Bill also lapsed. In the year 1985, another Lok Pal Bill was introduced in Lok Sabha on the pattern of the 1977 Bill. However the office of the Prime Minister was excluded from its purview. The Lok Pal was to be a single member body and its jurisdiction was confined to cases of corruption leaving out mal-administration and grievances. Be that as it may, this Bill also lapsed for the same reason as in the case of other such Bills. In the year 1989, another Lok Pal Bill was introduced. Under this, the Lok Pal was to be a three-member body and the office of the Prime Minister was also brought within its purview. There were some changes in the matter of eligibility for appointment and removal which it may not be necessary to mention here.

In the year 1996, yet another Lok Pal Bill was introduced in the Lok Sabha on 13th September, 1996. It was referred to the Department related Parliamentary Standing Committee on Home Affairs for examination. The Standing Committee submitted its report to the Parliament on 9th May, 1997. But before the government could finalize its thinking on the various recommendations of the Committee, the Lok Sabha was dissolved on 4 December 1997. Consequently, the Bill lapsed.

Another attempt at enacting the Lok Pal Act was made by the introduction of a Lok Pal Bill in the Lok Sabha on 3 August 1998, being Bill No. 90 of 1998. This Bill sought to provide for setting up the office of Lok Pal with a chairperson and two members with a fixed term. To ensure the members of their independence, it is provided that they shall not be removed from their office except by an order made by the President on the ground of proved misbehaviour or incapacity after an inquiry made by a committee consisting of the Chief Justice of India and two other judges of the Supreme Court, next to the Chief Justice in seniority, in which inquiry the member has been informed of the charges against him and given a reasonable opportunity of being heard in respect of those charges. The chairman and members are to be appointed by the President on the recommendation of the committee consisting of the Vice President of India (chairman), Prime Minister, Speaker of Lok Sabha, Minister of Home Affairs, Leader of the House to which the Prime Minister does not belong, Leader of the Opposition in the Lok Sabha and Leader of the Opposition in the Rajya Sabha. The jurisdiction of the Lok Pal under this Bill is to inquire into allegations constituting an offence punishable under the Prevention of Corruption Act, 1988. The Prime Minister, Union Ministers and Members of Parliament are within its purview. Clause 12 of the Bill provided that any person other than a public servant may make a complaint under that legislation to the Lok Pal (the expression 'complaint' is defined by sub-clause (c) to clause 2 to mean "a complaint alleging that a public functionary has committed any offence punishable under the Prevention of Corruption Act, 1988". The expression 'public functionary' means the Prime Minister, Union Ministers and Members of Parliament, both past and present). If it becomes necessary in the course of its inquiry, the Lok Pal is also empowered to inquire into any act or conduct of any person other than a public functionary insofar as it is necessary for an effective disposal of the matter within his jurisdiction. Clause 13 provides for preliminary scrutiny of complaints by Lok Pal whereas clause 14 provides for the procedure to be followed by Lok Pal in conducting any inquiry. Clause 15 clothes the Lok Pal with the power to summon any person or document from any person or authority. The Lok Pal is also vested with the powers of search and seizure by clause 16. Chapter IV of the Bill which contains only one clause, namely, clause 18, creates an obligation on every Member of Parliament to furnish a return of all assets owned by him and members of his family and all liabilities incurred by him and the members of his family, before the Lok Pal, within a period of 90 days from the date he enters upon his office and continue to do so every year within 90 days of the commencement of each financial year. The declaration has to be filed in the prescribed form. The expression 'family' is defined to include the spouse and dependent children of such member. This is certainly a defect. It would be more appropriate if the net is spread wider to include even major children and close relatives like father-in-law, mother-in-law, brothers, brothers-in-law and close associates.

While examining the provisions of the Bill, we have come to believe that while bringing the Prime Minister within the purview of the Lok Pal may be a desirable step, it is necessary at the same time to regulate and circumscribe that power. In our Constitutional system, i.e., under the parliamentary form of government, the Prime Minister occupies a unique position. He is the kingpin of the entire governmental structure. It is his image, his reputation and his personality that pervades the entire government. The image of the government is very often identified with the image of the Prime Minister. Because of the extraordinary power a Prime Minister wields in a parliamentary system like ours, it is sometimes referred to by jurists as 'prime ministerial form of government'. A Prime Minister is normally the leader of the majority party in the Lok Sabha or the leader of the coalition, if a coalition forms the government. Because of his very position and the power he wields, he attracts a good amount of opposition, criticism, allegations and what not. If a Lok Pal were to take up each and every allegation or accusation made against the Prime Minister by a political party or a group or a person, it would hobble the Prime Minister in an effective discharge of his functions. He cannot afford to remain under a cloud all the time nor can the nation afford a Prime Minister under a cloud all the time. Probably for this reason, in some of the earlier Bills, the Prime Minister was kept out of the purview of the Lok Pal. But, as we have said earlier, while it may be a desirable step to bring the Prime Minister within the purview of Lok Pal, it should at the same time be provided that before the Lok Pal undertakes any investigation, inquiry or any other proceeding against the Prime Minister, he should first obtain the permission in writing of the President therefor. It means that the Lok Pal shall place all the relevant material before the President and must satisfy the President with the facts and circumstances which call for an investigation and inquiry into those allegations and charges. The requirement of obtaining President's permission would be in the nature of a check upon a routine or mechanical initiation of inquiry by Lok Pal against the Prime Minister. One has to keep in mind in this behalf the distinction between legitimacy and legality. Legitimacy is a political concept. The Prime Minister normally represents the will of the majority of the people, being the leader of the majority of elected representatives. The legitimacy to rule belongs to him and his Council of Ministers. As against this, Lok Pal, a mere appointee, cannot be so empowered as to erode the image, reputation and personality of the Prime Minister by seeking to investigate or inquire into each and every allegation. The requirements of President's prior permission or sanction as it may be called would ensure that an investigation or inquiry into an allegation against the Prime Minister is taken up only where it is backed by substantial and acceptable evidence. The nation cannot afford to have a Prime Minister under a cloud, unless there are real and substantial grounds to believe that he may have been guilty of some serious misconduct. There is also a belief that the Prime Minister of a country should not be subjected to Lok Pal as this would severely impair his independence and freedom of judgement. The Prime Minister should have a free hand and absolute independence which is most necessary. Even if a particular Prime Minister is inclined that he should be subjected to Lok Pal, his readiness should not weigh with the Commission. There is a need to reconcile national interest and public interest and keeping in view how prime ministerial discretion is exercised, it would be a retrograde step. Anyhow, a new Bill titled The Lok Pal Bill, 2001 covering the Prime Minister also was introduced in Lok Sabha on 14th August, 2001.

In this connection, it would not be out of place to refer to the institution of the Independent Counsel created by Title VI of the Ethics in Government Act in USA. The Independent Counsel Act provides for appointment of an "independent counsel" to investigate and if appropriate prosecute certain high ranking government officials for violations of federal criminal laws. The Act requires the Attorney General, if he is satisfied on receipt of information that it is "sufficient to constitute grounds to investigate whether any person (covered by the Act) may have violated any federal criminal law", to conduct a preliminary investigation of the matter. When the Attorney General has completed this investigation, or 90 days has elapsed, he is required to report to a special court (the Special Division) created by the Act "for the purpose of appointing independent counsels". If the Attorney General determines that "there are no reasonable grounds to believe that further investigation is warranted", he must notify the Special Division of this result. In such a case, "the Division of the court shall have no power to appoint an independent counsel". If the Attorney General determines that there are "reasonable grounds to believe that further investigation or prosecution is warranted," then, he "shall apply to the Division of the court for the appointment of an independent counsel". The Attorney General's application to the court shall contain sufficient information to assist the court in selecting an independent counsel and in defining that independent counsel's prosecutorial jurisdiction. Upon receiving such information, the Special Division "shall appoint an appropriate independent counsel and shall define that independent counsel's prosecutorial jurisdiction".

The independent counsel's jurisdiction is very wide. He is vested with the full power and independent authority to exercise all investigative and prosecutorial functions and powers of the Department of Justice, the Attorney General and any other officer or employee of the Department of Justice. He can conduct grand jury proceedings and other investigations, he can participate in civil and criminal court proceedings and litigation and is also empowered to file appeals against any decision in any case in which he has participated in an official capacity. His powers include initiating and conducting prosecutions in any court of competent jurisdiction, framing and signing indictments, filing information and handling all aspects of any case in the name of the United States. He is entitled to call for assistance from any department or authority. Moreover, when a matter is referred to an independent counsel under the Act, the Attorney General in the Justice Department is required to suspend all investigations and proceedings with respect to the said matter. The validity of the Independent Counsel Act was challenged in the federal courts. The matter ultimately reached the United States Supreme Court. While a majority of seven judges led by Rehnquist C. J. upheld the validity of the Act holding that it does not curtail or infringe the powers of the President vested in him by clause 2 of section 2 of Article II of the U.S. Constitution, Scalia J. dissented (another Judge Kennedy J. took no part in the decision of the case)—Morrison v. Olson, 487 U.S. 654 (1988). Though the dissenting opinion of Scalia J. was criticized at that time as highly conservative, the events since then have proved him right. The manner in which an independent counsel appointed to investigate the Whitewater affair allegedly implicating President Bill Clinton and his wife was hijacked to take in unrelated issues is an instructive instance. Not able to find any substance against the President in the Whitewater issue, the Independent Counsel picked upon a case of suicide by a member of the White House staff and finding nothing therein shifted to Paula Jones' affair. While investigating the Paula Jones' affair, the independent counsel, Kenneth Starr, stumbled upon the Monica Lewinsky affair and everyone knows how the whole thing was blown up beyond all sensible and reasonable proportions leading to the impeachment proceedings and trial of President Clinton in Senate. The following observations of Scalia J. in the aforementioned case are pertinent:

"What every prosecutor is practically required to do is to select the cases for prosecution and to select those in which the offense is the most flagrant, the public harm the greatest, and the proof the most certain. If the prosecutor is obliged to choose his case, it follows that he can choose his defendants. Therein is the most dangerous power of the prosecutor; that he will pick people that he thinks he should get, rather than cases that need to be prosecuted. With the law books filled with a great assortment of crimes, a prosecutor stands a fair chance of finding at least a technical violation of some act on the part of almost everyone. In such a case, it is not a question of discovering the commission of a crime and then looking for the man who has committed it; it is a question of picking the man and then searching the law books, or putting investigators to work, to pin some offense on him. It is in this realm—in which the prosecutor picks some person whom he dislikes or desires to embarrass, or selects some group of unpopular persons and then looks for an offense, that the greatest danger of abuse or prosecuting power lies. It is here that law enforcement becomes personal, and the real crime becomes that of being unpopular with the predominant or governing group, being attached to the wrong political views, or being personally obnoxious to or in the way of the prosecutor himself... The mini-Executive that is the independent counsel, however, operating in an area where so little is law and so much is discretion, is intentionally cut off from the unifying influence of the Justice Department, and from the perspective that multiple responsibilities provide. What would normally be regarded as a technical violation (there are no rules defining such things) may in his or her small world assume the proportions of an indictable offense. What would normally be regarded as an investigation that has reached the level of pursuing such picayune matters that it should be concluded, may to him or her be an investigation that ought to go on for another year. How frightening it must be to have your own independent counsel and staff appointed, with nothing else to do but to investigate you until investigation is no longer worthwhile – with whether it is worthwhile not depending upon what such judgments usually hinge on, competing responsibilities. And to have that counsel and staff decide, with no basis for comparison, whether what you have done is bad enough, willful enough, and provable enough, to warrant an indictment... The notion that every violation of law should be prosecuted, including—indeed, especially—every violation by those in high places, is an attractive one, and it would be risky to argue in an election campaign that is not an absolutely overriding value. *Fiat justitia, ruat coelum.* Let justice be done, though the heavens may fall. The reality is, however, that it is not an absolutely overriding value....".

It is in the context of all the above circumstances, that we are inclined to suggest that there ought to be a proviso to clause 12 of the Lok Pal Bill in the following terms:

"Provided that before taking up any investigation or inquiry against the Prime Minister on the basis of any complaint or information received, the Lok Pal shall obtain the prior permission in writing of the President therefor."

Coming back to the Bill, it is difficult to predict whether the present Bill succeeds in becoming an Act or would it meet the same fate as its predecessors. But so far as it goes, the Bill is welcome though in certain respects it requires to be strengthened. The Bill rightly provides that a proceeding before the Lok Pal shall to be deemed to be a judicial proceeding within the meaning of section 193 of Indian Penal Code (clause 15(2)) and further that it is not necessary for the Lok Pal to maintain secrecy or other restriction upon the disclosure of information as provided in the Official Secrets Act, 1923 or any other provision of law. But, the Bill does not say that the conclusions arrived at by the Lok Pal shall be final and that if any public functionary is found guilty he should resign from his office including his membership of the Parliament/Legislature forthwith. Instead of doing that, section 17 merely speaks of the conclusions of the Lok Pal being communicated to the competent authority. (The expression "competent authority" is defined by sub-clause (b) in clause 2 of the Bill to mean (i) in the case of Prime Minister, the House of People; (ii) in the case of a member of the Council of Ministers other than Prime Minister, the Prime Minister and (iii) in the case of a Member of Parliament other than a minister, Rajya Sabha or Lok Sabha, as the case may be). Maybe, the Constitution may have to be amended to provide for an effective Lok Pal, with his own machinery of investigation.

Central Vigilance Commission

So far as the Central Vigilance Commission (CVC) is concerned, it has a long antecedent history. Pursuant to the recommendations of the Santhanam Committee constituted by the Government of India to advise the government in respect of matters pertaining to maintenance of integrity in administration, the CVC was established in 1964. The jurisdiction of CVC extended to all public servants and employees of central public sector undertakings, nationalized banks and autonomous organizations *vide* the resolution dated February 11, 1964 of the Government of India, Ministry of Home Affairs. It continued to function as such but without much effect until the Supreme Court directed in Vineet Narain vs. Union of India (1997 (7) SCALE 656) [AIR 1998 SC 889], on 18th December, 1997, to give a statutory shape to the CVC and to endow it with wider powers including supervision over Central Bureau of Investigation (CBI) and the Enforcement Directorate (ED). Indeed the Supreme Court, while giving the said directions had relied upon the report of the Independent Review Committee (IRC) comprising Shri B. G. Deshmukh, former Cabinet Secretary, Shri N. N. Vohra, Principal Secretary to the PM and Shri S. V. Giri, Central Vigilance Commissioner, which Committee was constituted under the Government Order dated 8th September, 1997. The directions of the Supreme Court are quite elaborate and they extend to the appointment, powers and functioning of CVC, CBI and ED, all designed to insulate the said institutions from political control and to invest them with good amount of independence coupled with accountability. (Those interested in perusing the said directions may refer to the aforementioned decision of the Supreme Court.) Pursuant to the said directions, the Central Government has drafted a Bill, being Bill No. 137 of 1999, called the Central Vigilance Commission Bill, 1999 and has introduced the same in Lok Sabha on 20 December 1999. It appears to be still pending before the Parliament. Meanwhile, the CVC is acting under the authority of the decision of the Supreme Court referred to above. It is imperative that the Parliament passes the said Bill as early as possible, keeping in mind the directions contained in the decision of the Supreme Court in Vineet Narain.

Civil Services Commission Board

An ancillary suggestion in this behalf that can be implemented without much ado, but which may have extremely beneficial results, is the constitution of a Civil Services Commission Board for overseeing appointment and transfer to senior posts. The idea is to take away the power of transfer from the political executive which, according to the universally held opinion, has not only been abused but has also been used in such a manner as to make the bureaucracy, including the IAS, plaint, toothless and corrupt. Maybe a Constitutional amendment is called for to provide for the composition of such a Board. The composition of the Board need not be exclusively non-political. It can be headed by the Prime Minister or the Home Minister and its jurisdiction restricted to certain high-level posts in the bureaucracy.

Suggestions of Central Vigilance Commission

Yet another ancillary idea floated by Shri N. Vittal, Central Vigilance Commissioner is to make the corruption-free governance, a fundamental right of the citizen. He has suggested that an article be inserted in Part III declaring such a right of the citizens. At any rate, Shri Vittal suggests, a provision to that effect must be included in Part IV (the Directive Principles of State Policy). He is of the opinion that such a provision would enable the Central and State Governments to legislate standards of probity and the rules governing the delivery of services to consumers of those services and in the matter of transfer of public employees. He is also of the opinion that insertion of such a right will provide an avenue for the civil society to demand transparency, fair procedures and decent behaviour on the part of the officials as also to demand public involvement in all matters affecting the public.

Ethics in Government Act of the United States of America

In this context, it would not be out of place to refer to certain provisions of the Ethics in Government Act enacted by the US Congress in 1978. Section 101 which carries the heading "persons required to file" says that (a) within 30 days of assuming the position of an officer or employee described in sub-section (f), an individual shall file a report containing the information described in section 102(b) unless the individual has left another position described in sub-section (f) within 30 days prior to assuming such new position or has already filed a report under this title with respect to nomination for the new position or as a candidate for the position. Sub-section (f) includes the President, the Vice President, each officer or employee in the executive branch, all government servants, members of the congress, officers or employees of the Congress, judicial officers and employees of the judiciary. Section 102 provides the matters which such declaration should contain.

It is a very lengthy section and it is not feasible to extract the whole of it. Suffice it to mention that the section provides for a full, true and complete disclosure of all kinds of assets including mortgages, movable assets, benefits under trusts and so on. Section 103 prescribes the time within which the report should be filed and the person before whom they should be filed. Section 104 empowers the Attorney General to bring a civil action in an appropriate US district court against any individual who knowingly and wilfully files a false declaration. Section 105 provides for custody of the declarations; it expressly provides that public shall have access to such declarations. Any US citizen is entitled to use the said reports for any lawful purpose. Section 106 provides for review and scrutiny of these reports by specified authorities. Section 108 declares that the Comptroller General shall have access to financial disclosure reports filed under the Act for the purpose of effectively discharging his statutory functions.

It is a matter for consideration whether it would be advisable for the Parliament to enact a legislation similar to the said U.S. Act.

G. Strengthening of the Criminal Judicial System

This is one of the most important requisites for ensuring probity in governance. The criminal judicial system consists of the police/investigating agency, the prosecuting agency, the advocates, witnesses and finally the judiciary. Inasmuch as this topic is dealt with in another paper, the same is not being dilated upon in this Consultation Paper.

❑❑❑

Official Secrets Act of India, 1923

4 APPENDIX

The Official Secrets Act, 1923 is India's anti-espionage act held over from British colonization. It states clearly that any action which involves helping an enemy state against India. It also states that one cannot approach, inspect, or even pass over a prohibited government site or area. According to this Act, helping the enemy state can be in the form of communicating a sketch, plan, model of an official secret, or of official codes or passwords, to the enemy. The disclosure of any information that is likely to affect the sovereignty and integrity of India, the security of the State, or friendly relations with foreign States, is punishable by this act.

Prosecution and Penalties

Punishments under the Act range from three to fourteen years imprisonment. A person prosecuted under this Act can be charged with the crime even if the action was unintentional and not intended to endanger the security of the state. The Act only empowers persons in positions of authority to handle official secrets, and others who handle it in prohibited areas or outside them are liable for punishment. In any proceedings against a person for an offence under this Act, the fact that he has been in communication with, or attempted to communicate with a foreign agent, whether within or without India is relevant and enough to necessitate prosecution. Journalists also have to help members of the police forces above the rank of the sub-Inspector and members of the Armed forces with investigation regarding an offence, up to and including revealing his sources of information (If required).

Under the Act, search warrants may be issued at any time if the magistrate feels that based on the evidence in front of them there is enough danger to the security of the state. Uninterested members of the public may be excluded from court proceedings if the prosecutions feels that any information which is going to be passed on during the proceedings is sensitive. This also includes media; so the journalists will not be allowed to cover that particular case. When a company is seen as the offender under this Act, everyone involved with the management of the company including the board of directors can be liable for punishment. In the case of a newspaper, everyone including the editor, publisher and the proprietor can be jailed for an offence.

❑❑❑